WHO'S ROXY WATKINS

SUSAN KEENE

Other Publications by Susan Keene

Finding Lizzy Smith (Kate Nash 1)
Tattered Wings
The Twisted Mind of Cletus Compton

Published by Bent Willow Books

ISBN 13: 978-0-9898831-7-7

ACKNOWLEDGMENTS

Thanks to Blenna for reading my work and giving great input.
Shirley McCann, you always do a great job, thank you.
Sharon Kizziah-Holmes, thank you for everything you do.

DEDICATION

In memory of
Molly Keene
July 3, 1970 – June 22, 2017
Forever in our hearts.

CHAPTER 1

The phone rang. I glanced at the caller ID before I answered it. The call came from Central. It couldn't be good. The clock on my bedside table flashed four a.m.

Homicide detectives from the St. Louis Major Case Squad called their office—*Central*. I hadn't been a detective with the force for over five years.

"Nash here," I answered.

"Kate, its Roger. I need you down here right away." We worked together in homicide for years. He was my partner and my friend since I left the department.

My feet were already on the floor. I scooted them around to find my slippers in the dark. "What's up? It's kind of early for a social call. Is there something I should know?"

"It's not personal. However, I do need you down here now."

My heart pounded in my ears. "Is that an order?"

He wasn't going to let this go. "I can send a car."

"Are you going to tell me what this is about?"

"I can't tell you over the phone. The most I can say is; it's imperative. Are you coming or should we come get you?"

"I don't like your tone, Roger."

"It's been a long night. I'll expect you within the hour." He hung up.

Jeez. I peed, brushed my teeth, and lassoed my unruly hair with a scrunchie. I picked up a St. Louis Cardinals sweatshirt and some jeans from the floor of my closet and put them on.

There were always more clothes on the floor and the dresser than ever got hung up or put away. One day I would straighten it up.

Chili, my two-year-old dachshund, slept peacefully on the bed. I gave her a pat on the head.

Ten minutes later, I headed downtown.

The parking lot was nearly empty. I drove up front and parked where all the cops left their personal cars and headed for the front door.

Roger leaned on a stair railing two steps above me. He came my way. "I need you to go in through the side door. Go directly to my office. Don't get sidetracked and don't talk to anyone."

"Come on, Roger; is this some sort of game?" I already knew it wasn't when I saw the way he looked at me."

I followed his wishes.

A couple of minutes later Roger walked in and sat. I saw the silhouette of a uniformed officer through the front door. I must have done something awful.

Roger sat in his chair behind the desk. The armed guard stepped into the room. I stood and looked from one of them to the other. The officer patted the back of my chair, to indicate I should sit again.

I did.

After a long pause, Roger broke the silence. "Where were you at twelve thirty this morning?"

"In bed asleep. I've had enough of this, do I need a lawyer?"

He picked up a pen and tapped it on his desk. "Do you? I haven't charged you with anything."

I tried to stand. The officer put his hand on my shoulder once again with enough pressure to persuade me to remain seated.

"Okay, enough's enough. We've been friends for almost ten years. If you and I have a problem you need to tell me what it is." I prefer to stand when I'm nervous. Roger knew that. It was an old interrogation technique. Make the subject as uncomfortable as possible. Get their mind on something else. They're more likely to answer with less thought. The fact he thought he needed to use it on me set me more on edge than I was before.

"Okay, Kate here goes. I have a dead body we picked up on the Delmar Loop and a dozen witnesses who say they saw you shoot him. There was a Saturday night showing of the cult film, The Rocky Horror Picture Show. The shooting took place in front of about a hundred people, but you know that, don't you Kate? They recognized you from the publicity after the Lizzy Smith case."

I didn't know whether to laugh or cry. I looked around for the camera that had to be recording this joke. All I could say was, "You've *got* to be kidding!"

Roger tossed the pen down. "That's what I thought. Before we called you down here we contacted every business in the area with a security camera. There were four, two on the movie theater. One pointed north and the second pointed south. One on the bank across the street recorded the shooting. Any detail it didn't show was picked up by the surveillance system on a nearby pharmacy."

I jerked myself away from the cop when he tried to stop me. I didn't care what they wanted; I would not sit another second. "You know I wouldn't shoot anyone without a reason and I'd call you immediately."

He nodded to the jailer behind me who walked over to a TV and turned it on.

Unbelievable! The woman on the tape was a dead ringer for me. She had the same red hair, same height and weight, and she dressed in my style. No wonder they dragged me down to the station.

Whoever she was, she walked up to a man. It appeared, from what I could see, they exchanged angry words. The man grabbed her and tried to drag her away. She broke free, pulled, what looked like a gun out of her jacket, and shot him several times. She took the time to lean down and take an object out of his pocket before she left.

This woman was bold. She strolled into the crowd as they left the movie. They parted like Moses at the Red Sea. She showed no urgency. Her demeanor was that of someone out for an evening stroll. She walked out of camera range. No one tried to stop her. It must have been a weapon in her hand. Why else would they appear intimidated? I stumbled back to the chair and plopped down before I passed out. I couldn't tell it wasn't me. "I know that looks incriminating, but it's not me. Can I see those tapes again?"

"Sure."

This time, now that the shock was over, I watched closer. The man walked up to her. He grabbed her by both wrists and tried to pull her in his direction. After she wiggled herself free she reached into her pocket. He took a huge step back. The man took three bullets to his chest. When it happened the woman turned to look at her. She hurriedly took something from his front jacket pocket, turned toward the movie theater and walked away. "When you look at it, really look at it, it looks like the shots came from behind her. I didn't see a gun in her hand, did you? Maybe the people in the movie crowd were stunned to see someone murdered in front of them and she didn't have a gun at all.

Roger stood, walked over and punched the off button. The tape stopped. "It gets better. She drove away in an older model BMW. What kind of car do you drive, Kate?"

Roger and the officer traded glances. "Come on, Kate. We both know it's you. I'm the first one who would try to believe any reasonable story you gave me. Maybe you have a twin sister."

"You know I'm an only child. Someone went to a lot of trouble to frame me for murder. I wouldn't be dumb enough to kill someone and use an old Beemer as my getaway car. We both know Michael gave me that car. He did most of the restoration work himself."

Michael was my husband who was murdered five years earlier.

Roger came around and sat on the corner of his desk. "You're right. I don't want to believe you killed anyone. I saw her look back like someone or something was behind her, and we can't definitively identify a weapon in her hand. All you have to do is tell me exactly what happened and you can go home."

I didn't say anything. I couldn't think of anything I could say to make it better.

"In my heart, I can't believe you killed someone in cold blood; or otherwise. Since you can't tell me about it, and you can't prove you were home asleep, I'm going to book you. Don't look at me like that Kate. I have a lot of people to answer to. I'd lose my job if I let you walk out of here. I took the liberty of notifying Ryan. I thought you might need moral support. Meanwhile, you can cool your heels in holding. By the way, there are reporters outside trying to find out what happened. You're famous Kate. I know you didn't want to be, but you are."

I rested my head in my hands for a few seconds and rubbed my eyes. "Who was the man?"

Roger stood. "All we know right now, I learned from what he carried in his pockets. He wore a Giorgio Armani suit and Bally shoes. You're talking a lot of money. His name was Tony De Grasse, forty years old. There was a .357 Magnum on the ground next to him. Was it yours, Kate? What did you take out of his pocket? His driver's license indicated he lived in New Jersey. He had a rap sheet with many arrests and no convictions. It looks like he might have been with the Mafia. Does any of this make sense to you?"

The door opened and there stood my boyfriend, Ryan. I wondered how much Roger had told him.

I don't know if I was more angry or scared. People went to prison for life on less evidence than what they had on me. I walked to Ryan. He opened his arms and I tried to disappear into his embrace.

"Did they tell you they're charging me with…?" I turned to Roger. "What are the charges?"

He nodded a greeting to Ryan and answered. "Manslaughter two, armed criminal action, illegal use of a firearm, so far, the DA will review the case. He might amend it."

I stepped back and put my hands on my hips. "That's crazy. I have my weapon on me and it hasn't been fired. I've always carried a Glock 19. You know that. Ryan gave me a look I interpreted as—*don't say another word.*

CHAPTER 2

A woman officer took my gun, cell phone, socks, jewelry, and the rubber band from my hair before she led me to a holding cell. The only good thing about the situation was they didn't take me to the county jail and stick me in with the general population. I had the six by eight feet cell to myself in the safety of the police station.

Ryan pulled a chair up to the bars and sat so we could talk. "I go out of town for three days and you get in trouble."

"I understand you're trying to lighten the mood Ryan, but it's not going to happen. They let you see the tape. She looks like me."

Ryan and I had been friends since college. We got closer after the murder of my husband. Our problem remained the same from day one. Because Michael was dead, didn't mean I had stopped loving him.

For the most part, Ryan and I had a great relationship. If could stop my feelings for my dead husband, I could make the final commitment to him. Thank goodness, he didn't push.

He stood and backed away. "Don't say anything to Roger, but there's a message on the apartment phone. It's from a woman with a distinct Eastern accent. She let me know she was sorry for the trouble she caused. She didn't kill anyone, and she'll make this up to you."

I leaned against the bars. "What do you think that means? It must be the woman in the video."

"At this point it's hard to say what's going on. I need for Neil to take a look at the tapes before you see a judge. But they'll only hand them over to your attorney. With your permission, I'll call James King to represent you. They'll give the tapes to him."

Neil was Ryan's tech guy and James King was his personal attorney.

I looked at my watch which wasn't there. "Sure, whatever it takes. When were you at the apartment?"

"About an hour ago. Roger called while I was still on the plane, but I wanted to take my luggage home and I knew Chili would be alone"

"Oh, how is she? Did you feed her?"

"Yes I took her out to potty, fed her, and covered her up on the couch. She was snoring when I left. We don't have much time to come up with something to get you out of here." He reached through the bars and took my hand. "I don't think you'll do well in jail. We need to find something on the tapes to exonerate you. I have my men working on finding out who the man was and why he was so far from home. Roger had information but I want more."

I stuck my hands in my pockets. "His name was Tony De Grasse. He had on a four thousand dollar suit and thousand dollar pair of shoes. He was from New Jersey. That's all I know."

Ryan took the notepad he always carried in his pocket, opened it and read. "Those are the same facts he gave me. Before I left his office he said they found a new Lincoln three blocks from the body. It's registered to a Dominic De

Marco. It was clean as a whistle and had New Jersey plates. Does the name De Marco mean anything to you?"

I put my fingers on top of his. "First, James is fine and no I'm not familiar with the name. I'll mentally go through the last cases we have tackled and see if I remember anyone like you described. Amy might remember something."

"De Marco runs the biggest crime family in the east."

Ryan left, within twenty minutes, he was back with James King. James stepped near the barred door with a piece of paper in his hand. "Kate, sign this affidavit. It gives me the right to represent you. It'll force Roger to turn over all the evidence and I'll share it with Ryan."

I reached through the bars, took the paper in one hand, a pen he offered in the other. I walked over to the far wall, used it for a writing surface, and signed my name. As soon as I handed it back to him, he left. I forgot to say thanks.

Ryan stood as close as he could to me and held out his hand. I readily took it. "I called Amy so she wouldn't worry. She'll go to the apartment and pick up the dog. Chili will be better off with her and Digger. That way if we get tied up, she won't be alone. Do you want anything?"

Amy was my best friend and business partner. Digger was her spoiled Yorkie, who she treated like a child. There was a time when I wouldn't have understood the pet and owner bond.

After a particularly bad case, Ryan bought me the dog. I figured it was so I would be forced to focus on something besides the guilt I had after the case was settled.

"No. I am fine. I need for this to be over."

James came back with copies of the videos in hand. He gave one to Ryan. Both men promptly left.

I knew Ryan to be a brilliant man, but I couldn't imagine how he could fix this. There wasn't anything for me to do but worry and stare at the large office clock on the other side of the room. Officers came and went. No one paid any attention to me; the prisoner in the holding cell at the far corner of the room.

It was my habit when something didn't go my way, to find a quiet place, close my eyes and try to picture every scene of the event like a slide show. There was a lot of noise in the police station, but it was all I had. I went back in my mind to cases six months old and followed my interactions up to the last week. I came up empty.

Roger brought me a latte and a bagel with cream cheese. I smiled my biggest and most sincere smile. I had this breakfast almost every day of my life. Finally, something I could feel positive about.

"I looked at today's docket. It's a busy one. You're not on the schedule until about six o'clock tomorrow evening. It'll give Ryan more time to try to find a loophole in this. You know, Kate...?

I stopped him. "Yes, Roger. I know you're doing your job. I'll have to hope the system works in my favor." I sipped my latte.

"It's perplexing. The woman on the tape looks like you. I don't doubt you, but it's pretty incriminating." He stopped talking when Amy walked up and stood beside him.

"Hi, Kate. Are you okay? Ryan filled me in. It doesn't seem possible. Maybe you have a doppelganger."

Roger nodded to both of us and walked toward his office.

I munched on the bagel. "I'm not familiar with the term, what is it?"

"It's your double. They say everybody has one. If I have one, I hope she isn't a criminal." She raised a bag so I could see it. "Where'd you get the food? I have the same thing for you right here."

"Roger brought it, but I'll take more. It sounds like I'll be here a long time. I need to pee so badly, but I refuse to go. I might as well be in the lobby at Union Station." I looked around. There were at least eight people roaming around the room. No one paid any attention to me, but they could at any minute. "This is horrible."

Amy opened her coat as wide as it would go and put her back to the bars. "Go ahead. I'll shield you from prying eyes."

I smiled a little. "Thanks. How embarrassing, one of the things that always kept me from being a crook; no privacy." There was a small sink with a soap dispenser next to it. I scrubbed my hands, but the paper towel holder was empty so I dried them on my jeans. "Why are you here? I thought you would be home with our puppies."

Amy reached for the camera we used in our work. "I was. Ryan called. He needs pictures of both your hands from every angle. He wants me to take close-ups."

"Why?"

She shrugged. "He didn't say. He told me what pictures he wanted and where he wanted me to take them to get them developed. Silver Screen Photo is waiting for me now. The tech is to blow them up as large as possible. One of his men will meet me there to pick them up."

I stuck my hands through the bars. She took a dozen pictures of each of them.

I shook my head. "So, Ryan didn't give you a clue about what he has in mind?"

She winked at me. "No, but I do know if there's some way we can get you out of here, we will. You hang on and don't worry about anything. I moved our appointment with the *theft lady* from this afternoon to a week from Tuesday."

I smiled at her. There was really nothing more to say. I'd forgotten about the case we had the next afternoon.

The rest of the night, I lay on the small cot in the cell. It had a cold plastic covering, no sheet, no pillow, and no blanket.

CHAPTER 3

The courtroom was as packed as a can of expensive sardines. The seats from the center to the railing were filled with petty criminals, drug dealers, and juveniles who waited for arraignment. To the left were lawyers, and to my surprise, reporters filled the gallery in the back of the room. I looked around to see who warranted the press. It didn't take but a moment to realize I was the person of interest. I didn't see Ryan, Amy, or my attorney.

In all fairness, I was the girlfriend of Ryan Meade one of St. Louis's rich and elite. Only a couple of people had made the papers more than him and me. We made front-page news last year when we uncovered the mystery of a triple homicide and kidnapping. The media kept that story alive day after day for more than a month. They hungered for more.

Ryan and his group walked in and reporters shouted questions. The judge banged his gavel on the desk a few times and screamed something about clearing the courtroom. It got quiet again.

I sat and stared straight ahead. I had to sit forward without the comfort of the back of the chair because of the handcuffs. They held my wrists securely behind me.

Each case only took minutes. The judge listened, fined, sentenced, set court dates, and shook his head in disgust. He handled ten to fifteen cases in half-an-hour. Only one case had been dismissed. It seemed hopeless.

When the bailiff called my name, I tried my best to stand. As short as I was, there was no room to get my feet under me. I need not have worried. A guard walked over and helped me to my feet. He unfastened the cuffs and redid them so my hands were in front of me.

Jim King came through the gate at the front at the same time as I did. He took my arm and led me to a table on the other side. It separated the defendants who waited from those who were next. We didn't sit.

"Kathleen Madison Nash?" The judge looked around the courtroom as if he didn't see us while we stood directly in front of him.

"She is here, Your Honor."

The judge looked up. "One count of second-degree manslaughter, one count assault with a deadly weapon, one count of unlawful use of a firearm, how do you plead?"

"Not guilty." My lawyer answered for me.

The judge tilted his head down and looked at us over the top of his half glasses. "The defendant needs to speak for herself, Counselor."

"Not guilty," I affirmed in my loudest voice. If the judge thought it was an act of rebellion, he didn't say.

"Well, Mr. King. We don't see you down here often, did you get bored or are you slumming? Careful you don't get your shoes dirty." He paused. When he didn't get a reaction, he continued. "The State is asking one million dollars bail and for Mrs. Nash to surrender her passport."

"Judge, we can prove beyond a shadow of a doubt that Mrs. Nash was not the person who perpetrated this crime."

Before Jim finished his sentence, the roar in the courtroom thundered.

His Honor hammered on the table again. "This is not a trial, Mr. King. You can't present evidence in my court. The one and only issue here is should Mrs. Nash be allowed to go free on bond until her court date."

"Kate, sorry, Kathleen, is not a flight risk and is a pillar of the community. She's a business owner and a well thought of member of St. Louis society," Jim asserted.

"Even more troubling, Counselor. Do you carry a weapon in your profession, Mrs. Nash?"

I shook my head *yes*.

"I can't hear you. The defendant needs to speak up."

My face flushed. The heat started in my toes and skyrocketed to my head. "Yes, sir, I do indeed carry a weapon," I answered in a sharp, clear voice.

He slammed the mallet on the top of the desk once and announced. "I'm ready to rule. Bail is set at one million dollars, cash or bond. The defendant will relinquish her gun, her Private Investigation License, as well as her passport until this matter is settled. This defendant will be held in the County Jail."

"Judge, you're tying Mrs. Nash's hands and making it impossible for her to make a living." A murmur passed through the crowd.

"Take it or leave it, Mr. King. My first inclination was no bail, so you're a lucky man. Next case: Darrell James Simpson."

He was done with us.

CHAPTER 4

They ushered me out a side door. It didn't look good. It meant I needed to go through central booking and lock-up at the county jail.

Once I became a prisoner, things would move at a snail's pace. No telling how long before I could see or talk to anyone. Jeez. What a mess.

I need not have worried. I didn't get as far as the transport van before Ryan showed up with all the paperwork to free me. I heard a guard tell him to go on to the jail. We would be there soon and if the paperwork was in order they would let me go.

Ryan walked toward me. One of the guards held a baton in front of his chest to stop him. "You're not allowed within twenty-feet of the prisoners."

Ryan turned on his heel and left without a backward glance. I could only hope things would go well.

We sat on the curb and waited for prisoners for another four hours. No one cared about our well being. As a case was disposed of, the defendant went in one of three vans—one went to the county jail, one to the mental ward at Barnes-

Jewish Hospital and the other to Fulton, the state prison. They had it all worked out.

Even though the trip to the jail shouldn't have taken more than thirty minutes, it took another two hours. One man, who looked like he'd slept in his clothes for weeks and smelled like whiskey and dirty socks, threw up all over the van. The other men, I was the only female, raised such a ruckus, the guards stopped and hosed out the vehicle.

I learned more about prisoner transport than I ever cared to.

We walked single file into the foyer of the facility. Someone called my name. I was unshackled from the men in front of me and behind me. A big woman took my arm, not too gently, and pushed me into a room on my left. Ryan and Jim were there.

Once we were in she shoved me toward them and slammed the door. "She's free to go."

I couldn't hold back the tears. I'm not a crier, but exhaustion, the thought of spending more time in a cell, and lack of food and sleep had gotten the best of me.

Ryan helped me into his truck—I was greeted by my beautiful fur-baby, Chili. Best decision ever. I loved that dog. She listened to all of my complaints, joys, and sorrows, and loved me no matter how I looked, acted, or sounded.

Ryan stood outside and talked to Jim for a few minutes. I didn't care. I folded my legs under me, turned the heater on full blast, closed my eyes, and hugged my dog. Thank goodness part of my nightmare was over.

Ryan opened the door on his side and slid into the driver's seat. "I hope you're getting warm."

I reached to turn down the heat. "Oh, I'm sorry."

"No. It's fine. What're you hungry for?"

"Steak 'n Shake; a double cheeseburger and an orange freeze." Once a few bites of warm, comfort food hit my stomach and the heat in the truck reached my core, I felt human again. I hoped a hot shower and a good night's sleep was the answer.

"I can't believe you put up that much money for bail."
He was shamelessly rich. Only two people in the area had
more money. One owned a brewery and the other a rental car
company. Ryan inherited his, but he never forgot how
blessed he was. He had his hand in art galleries, restaurants,
real estate, a semi-pro basketball team, and owned the largest
home and business security company in the Midwest.

He pulled me to him and hugged me and Chili at the
same time. "Honey, its only paper. You aren't going to skip
the country are you?"

"No." I reached over and touched his leg. "They took
my passport." We both chuckled. "I'm worried about how
I'm going to live with no license to work and no gun."

He put his hand on mine. "Kate, don't worry about it.
I'll take care of everything,"

"I know you want to, but let me ask you a question." I
didn't wait for him to say anything. "What do they call a
woman who sleeps with a man, doesn't work, and lets him
support her? Before you answer let me tell you, I know about
fifty words for her and none of them are flattering."

He glanced down at me. "You're being a little hard on
yourself, aren't you?" He pulled to the curb and put the truck
in park.

I held Chili tighter. "This could go on for a long time. I
have no gun, no credentials, and not much money. It doesn't
look promising."

He took my hand in his and patted it. "Here's my idea.
Finish your burger. Take a hot shower and sleep until you
feel better. Amy and I have a plan. If it works, and Jim
thinks it will, I'll have you cleared by the end of the week.
We've done all we can do at the moment." He leaned toward
me. We shared a tender kiss and headed home.

CHAPTER 5

I woke up with Chili's tongue up my nose. She wanted to go outside to potty. For the hundredth time in the past few weeks, I thought I needed to move out of my penthouse apartment overlooking Forest Park. When nature called and I wanted to take her outside I had to keep her on a lead. She never got to run free.

The apartment served me well over the years. It, along with a paid lease, was a wedding gift to Michael and me from Ryan. I stayed because of the memories of Michael and because it was paid for. I didn't need four bedrooms and three baths. I needed a backyard with a fence. As soon as I could work again, I would search for a house on a quiet street with a huge fenced backyard.

When I went back inside there was a missed call on my cell phone. Caller ID read Ryan Meade, but he didn't leave a message. I called back anyway. "Hi, you called?"

"Yes. Can you be ready to go to Jim's office for a meeting in about thirty minutes? I'm sorry it's short notice, but I wanted to let you sleep as long as possible."

It was mid-morning already. "Sure, I'll be ready and downstairs in thirty."

I fed Chili, filled her water bowl, and stroked her back while she ate. I took another shower to try to get the smell and memories of the jail cell off me. I looked around for something to wear. Someday I intended to go through my closet, throw away what I no longer wore. I thought it about once a week. When the time came, I could find a thousand other things I had to do.

When I looked in the mirror, I didn't always have self-acceptance. I was too short, my hair unruly and my boobs tiny. But no one had ever tried to put a bag over my head because they couldn't stand to look at me, so all was not lost.

I liked dresses but hardly ever wore one. In my line of work, I ran, jumped, ducked and pushed on a regular basis. Slacks, feminine tops and tailored blazers to hide my weapon were my uniforms. Spike heels were my trademark. Anything I could do to make me taller than my five feet one inch and made me look more imposing on the job.

I slipped on a little black dress with no jacket. Ryan must have thought the dress was a good choice. He whistled when the elevator door opened and I stepped out.

We arrived at Jim's posh Clayton law office about ten minutes later. Amy and my nail technician, Debbie, were there. I mouthed *hi* on my way by.

An assistant ushered Ryan and me into James's office and closed the door. Jim worked a few more seconds on something on his desk and looked up with a cheesy grin. "I think we have it."

Ryan smiled, "Good."

"Would you guys like to clue me in? I want to be happy too."

"Okay, the grand jury's in session. Your case goes before them within the next three weeks. But, it will never go to court. I called Darrin Donavan and made an appointment with him for tomorrow."

Darrin Donavan was the district attorney for St. Louis County. There were several of them but Darrin led the pack. "I assured him we have proof you're not the woman in the video. At first he laughed then he laughed and said; "The video I saw gives me an ironclad case." James picked up some pictures that had been lying on his desk. "Look at these, Kate. Do you recognize them?"

"Yes. The ones on the right are the pictures of my hands Amy took at the jail the other night."

"And the other pictures?" He wanted to know.

I shook my head. "I haven't a clue."

"The other pictures are enlargements of the hands of the woman in the video. They prove beyond a doubt it's not you on those tapes."

I was skeptical. "How can you prove it?"

"That's why Amy and Debbie Crawford are here. Amy will testify your hands looked like these pictures hours after the crime. Debbie will testify she does your nails every other Tuesday and has for the last four years." He put the other pictures on top. "This woman hasn't had her nails done in the recent past. What else do you see?" Before I could answer he continued, "When they locked you in the holding cell you removed your jewelry. Look at your hands. You have deep white lines where your rings were. She doesn't. Believe me, it's enough to finish this entire thing."

Ryan sat quietly through out the exchange He leaned over and patted my hand. "It's enough."

Jim took another long look at the photos as he restacked them. "There are other differences in your hands and hers. I don't think we'll need them. Darrin will drop the case and this will be behind you. Believe me, Kate."

"And you are sure?" It seemed like a long shot to me.

James put the pictures in a manila envelope and slapped it with the back of his hand. "The district attorney won't take this to the grand jury for an indictment. Those men have large egos. No one wants to take a case to court they can't win. This one would command a great amount of publicity. He'd be foolish to continue once he sees these."

I let out the breath I didn't realize I'd been holding. "Thanks, that's wonderful. Now we only have one problem."

"What's that?" Both men talked at once.

"What keeps her from doing it again—or something worse? Who is she? I don't mind telling you, I'm nervous."

CHAPTER 6

I picked my gun and credentials up on Friday afternoon. Ryan told me it was over. But I knew the other shoe would fall one day. I was sure of it.

The thing about publicity is that it didn't matter if it was good or bad. Amy and I had more new business than we could handle. Never in our career were we able to pick and chose from so many cases.

We picked a woman, Nancy Trimble, who had bought a condo from a fellow who was now her maintenance man. She was convinced every time she left her home, he went in and moved things around.

Our appointment with her was after lunch. We had Digger and Chili with us. They went with us if the temperatures weren't too hot or cold. They were happy campers and comfortable in the truck while we visited with our client. Many times when we came back, they were burrowed together under a blanket I kept in the back seat.

Mrs. Trimble answered the door. "Are you from the" When she got to detective agency, she looked around and whispered the words.

Amy handed her our card. "Yes, I'm Amy Perkin and this is Kate Nash, may we come in?"

She stepped away from the door and gave us room to enter. Before she closed it she stuck her head out and looked in both directions.

The room was overstuffed with collectibles. There were figurines of dogs, cats, Friar Folk, Sister Folk, elephants, tigers, donkeys, and Precious Moments statues. I didn't have to move to see the dining room was filled with tiny mouse figurines, mules, elephants, and squirrels. It was all I could see from where I stood. I had the impression we'd stepped into an entire house full of what I referred to as dust catchers.

It would take an amazing memory for anyone to know if an item had been moved. Every tabletop, counter, the television, and numerous shelves had some sort of collection.

Amy walked around the room. "Do you know where everything in this room is placed?"

She went to a cabinet near where Amy stood. "My first husband gave me everything in here and on the piano. The things in the bedroom belonged to Mother. All the rest was given to me by my second husband, Wilbur."

I sat on the couch and opened the little notebook I carried in my back pocket. "When did you first find something in the wrong place?"

She sat beside me. "I've been uneasy ever since I bought this apartment last June. Something is not right around this complex. I can't put my finger on it. Last month I noticed when I left and came back, my collections would be out of place."

Amy sat in a chair that faced us. "Can you give me a for instance?"

She looked from Amy to me. "The first time, six of my Persian cats were gone from their shelf. They were over there with the German Short Hairs. I would never mix the cats and dogs for fear one of them would be injured.

"I left to grocery shop. When I arrived home, my Precious Moments figures were in disarray. Some of them were in the other room with the Hummels. The two sets of statues don't get along. There's a lot of jealousy between them. I find a different arrangement of my lovelies each time I come back from an outing."

I wrote it down. Maybe someone wanted to mess with her mind or force her to move. "What would you like us to do?"

She put her hand over her mouth in an, *oh my* gesture. "I was certain you would know what to do to stop this. If you don't, I have no idea what the answer is."

"We know what to do, Mrs. Trimble. We generally like to ask our clients what they expect so we are on the same page."

She looked relieved. "I'm glad to hear it. When could you start?"

"We are going to familiarize ourselves with the complex now. Tomorrow morning we will begin."

There were miniatures of cooking items, ranges, and tiny utensils in the kitchen. Her bedroom, except for a path to her bed and the master bath, held at least forty quilts. They were on racks, walls, stacked on the dresser, the bedside table and hung from ceiling to floor in two places.

The guest bedroom housed holiday-themed items. Christmas trees decorated with lights, ornaments, and garland, a group of angels graced the top of the dresser and chest, and there were many tree skirts spread on the bed as if they were blankets. It was a sight to behold. She hadn't ignored Halloween, Easter, Independence Day, New Years, Memorial Day, Martin Luther King, Jr. Day, or George Washington's Birthday. It was an assault on the senses.

"I only see one door in and out. Is that correct?" I asked.

"Yes. It's one of the things I like. Once I secure the front door, I have no worries that anyone will bother me."

Amy walked to the front hallway. "Do you have a schedule of your appointments and outings for the next week, or at least the next few days? It would be best if you were out and about."

"Yes, yes, of course. I have a medical check-up, bridge club, mid-week church, and if you haven't caught the culprit, I can add more. I want to thank you ladies. I have every confidence you will put a stop to this."

On the way to the car, I glanced toward Amy. "How many pieces do you think are in there?"

"While the two of you went over the paperwork, I counted four hundred and eighteen in the one curio cabinet next to the kitchen. I'd estimate five to six thousand, maybe more."

I shook my head. "Except for clothes and shoes, I'm a minimalist."

Our conversation ended when we got to the truck. The puppies acted like we'd been gone for weeks. We gave them all our attention.

We arrived at the condo at eleven the next morning. Our client needed to be at her card game at noon. I snacked on an apple while Amy read about living full time in an RV. "Are you interested in that?"

"No. My Aunt Alice wants to retire and drive around the country. It sounds like work to me."

Our conversation was cut short when we spotted Mrs. T, as she headed for her car. Since there was only one way in and one way out of her place, there were dozens of places we could park to observe the door. If we sat too long in one place, someone was bound to complain.

Time dragged. Amy walked Digger. "Didn't she say, *every time she left?*"

"Yes, she did." I took Chili for a walk; there was still no sign of anyone around the place. Once I sat in front of the swimming pool and Amy went to the balcony so she could look down on the situation. No matter how many times we changed our vantage point, nothing happened at the apartment.

Not only did no one go near Nancy Trimble's apartment, not many people wandered around. Meals on Wheels delivered to a few apartments. There was a carpet cleaner, the

Dish man, and the mailman who filled the boxes at the edge of the parking lot.

Promptly at three-thirty she was back. We drove to our office. Amy gave her a call. "Nothing's out of place today, right?"

"Why yes, my Hummels are no longer in alphabetical order." Amy put her hand over the receiver. "Her Hummels are out of order." She looked at me and shrugged her shoulders.

"Tell her not to move anything. We'll be back in the morning to assess the damage."

This went on for several more days. She would leave, we would watch, no one would go into her apartment but she always found something out of place. We decided to split up the next day. I sat where I could see the kitchen window. Only an acrobatic person with the ability to jump fifteen feet in the air could get in. Nothing happened. Our client let us in to take a better look around.

I was in the kitchen while Amy looked through the bedroom with Mrs. Trimble. I called to them. "Can you come in here?" I pointed to a piece of aluminum foil taped on the range vent, two pieces were wrapped around the stove vent and another taped to the front of the radio. "I don't remember these being here before. What are they for?"

"I put them there so no one can hear me."

Amy moved in front of her "So who can't hear you? Do you have nosey neighbors?"

"No— *them*." I could barely hear her.

I pulled a chair out from under the kitchen table and suggested she sit. Amy and I sat across from her. "Tell us who *they* are."

"The people who don't live on this planet, you know— the aliens."

Amy leaned forward and put her hand on Nancy's arm. "Is the maintenance man one of *them*?"

"I don't think so, he seems normal, but he must have an invisibility cloak so you can't see him come in. How else could he move my things?"

"Have you ever seen him put on his invisibility cloak and disappear?"

"No, I haven't, but there's no other possible answer."

"I see. In that case Mrs. Trimble, you are wasting your money paying us to watch the condo. Why don't we make this our last day? He has the advantage because of the cloak. Most likely he won't allow us to see him. I think you'll be fine if you put your things back where they belong when you get home. Some of those technical helpers like the cape and their listening devices are too advanced for us."

"Are you sure? I watched a documentary on life around the galaxy. The host commented that there could be as many as a thousand or more civilizations besides ours."

Amy leaned forward. "Not all the things you watch on television are real."

"This one was. It played every night on the public station. They are a teaching station; they wouldn't spend that much time on something that wasn't true."

Amy opened her mouth to say something else. I shook my head no. I guessed our client to be well into her eighties. I didn't want to demean or destroy her over this.

We were quiet until we got in the car. Amy looked at me. "What do you think?"

"I believe she thinks it's all true. She has no family left. She might spend too much time alone or maybe she gets confused. Let's call around and get someone to come out and see her."

We called The Council on Aging, The Senior Center, the mental ward at the hospital and the Mental Clinic over on Delmar.

A month later a lady called and told us we might want to know our aging friend was better. The social worker added that Mrs. Trimble still insisted someone moved her things each time she left her apartment.

CHAPTER 7

Roger called a little after midnight. "Well, Kate seems like your double has been spotted."

"Jeez Roger, do I have to come in again?"

"No, at the time she was seen you were at an art gallery opening with Ryan. I have eyewitness accounts from at least twenty folks. They saw her or you at a grocery store, a liquor store, and a flower shop. We have the number of the taxi that picked her up and the address where it dropped her off."

"What did she do?"

"She didn't do anything. Remember, she's a suspect in a homicide. The report came back on our victim. Initial reports were correct. He was connected. Wonder what she, personally, has to do with organized crime?"

"Roger, I don't like this. I could get hurt if I go out and get mistaken for her. I could get shot or worse."

I heard him take a sip of something—most likely coffee from the filthy pot in his office. I was sure it hadn't been cleaned since I left.

"I thought of that too. Keep your head down. Maybe you'd like to go along when I track down the address she gave the cabbie."

"Sure, sure I would. I'll be right down."

"No need. I'll pick you up".

Ryan came through the bathroom door with wet hair and a towel tied around his waist. "Who was that at this hour?"

"Roger, it seems my look-alike was out on the town tonight."

He sat next to me on the bed. We had gotten home late and he wanted to stay over. Of course, I said yes. "We need to spend some time on this. They say everyone has a doppelganger, yours happens to be a criminal."

"Which reminds me, I'm going to ride along with him. We're going to the address she gave a cab driver tonight."

"What do you think she'll do when she sees you?"

"She knows all about me or she wouldn't have called the apartment and left a message when I was in jail."

"Yes, I bet she does. Be careful."

"Ryan, you're telling me that you're not going to ask to go along?"

He slipped on some pajama pants and slid under the covers. "I'm tired and I need to read this report before I go to sleep. You go and have fun."

He kissed me lightly on the lips.

I got into Roger's unmarked car and he drove us to the far south side of the city.

I loved it there. The homes were close together and went upward instead of outward. I went in one of them years ago to investigate a murder. They were narrow, with one room on each floor. Each bathroom had a floor of its own. At one time it was a Dutch community with families at every address. As population aged it became a posh area for Generation X.

We stopped in front of the address the cab company gave the police. It was a shell of a building. When they renovated the home they tore it all down except the front which they used as a false facade. They did it to keep the character of the old neighborhood.

I read the address I had in my hand. "2707 Lafayette, this should be it. Want to go a block in each direction and see if she's around?"

"No Kate, I don't. Look around, this construction goes on for miles in each direction. In the morning I'll send some patrolmen to scout around. She's not only keeping her whereabouts secret from us, she's running from the mob. The fact that she has lived into her thirties is a testament to her resources. Sorry I drug you out on this chilly night to chase a ghost."

"That's all right. It was a nice diversion."

We drove back to the Penthouse in silence.

I got off the elevator at three-thirty. Chili came out of the bedroom stretching and reluctantly walked to me. "Were you asleep little girl?" She wagged her tail and moseyed toward the kitchen where I kept her water bowl. She was back in a second. "Ready to go back to bed?" She jumped up on her hind legs so I could pick her up.

The bedroom was dark, but Ryan had left a light on in the bathroom. I sat the dog on the bed. She tunneled under the covers. For several moments I listened to Ryan breathe. I admitted to myself how much I loved him.

I went to sleep but I didn't stay asleep. A dream woke me. My double could become invisible and kept appearing and disappearing through the microwave.

It turned into a long night. I woke starving. Ryan went to get lattes and bagels with cream cheese while I stood in the shower until the water ran cool.

He took Chili with him and included a long walk around the block in the deal. I thought again how I wanted a house on the ground floor with a fence so I could let the dog roam.

I needed to meet Amy at the office at one o'clock to discuss our next case. Jake, Amy's boyfriend, who played baseball for the Springfield Cardinals, was in town. She wasn't in any hurry to get to work.

I turned on my laptop and looked up doppelganger.

Doppelganger: a person who is a double for another, considered a physic phenomenon. It is used in literature as a case for mistaken identity.

Lovely.

There was story after story of these look-a-likes. One told of a teacher who was in the classroom yet people saw her in the garden at the same time. Another talked about a poet whose double sat down across from him and proceeded to dictate the exact poem he had written.

I couldn't believe that was what happened to me.

I met Ryan at the elevator. "Are you busy today?"

He handed me a bagel. "I have some phone calls to make. Give me an hour and I'm yours for the day."

"I want to go over the surveillance tapes from the places Miss X went last night. I thought maybe you'd like to go along."

"Sure, aren't you supposed to meet Amy?"

"Yes, but Jake's in town and she's taking the morning off. I'll check in with her later."

He leaned over and gave me a peck on the cheek. "Okay, finish your breakfast and I'll be done as soon as possible." He reached in his pocket for his phone, punched in a number, walked over to the dining room table to talk."

An hour later, we were in the crime lab watching tapes with one of the techs. I had to admit, in every way she was me; hair, eyes, coloring, and some mannerisms.

It all made me antsy. I asked the tech. "I know doppelgangers are a psychic phenomena, But do you know anything about them?"

"Being with the police department, I most usually look at people, dead and alive. So the look-a-like issue fascinates me. A photographer by the name of Fransous Brunelle put an advertisement in the newspaper asking for anyone who knew people who looked alike. He thought there would be one or two at the most. At last count, he had photographed over fifteen hundred doubles. When I say they look alike, I am discounting twins. That was about ten years ago. I read an article saying he had a contract with a publishing company to turn his photos into a coffee table book."

Ryan and I shared a glance of disbelief. "I don't think this woman is my double. I think she's either some nut-job who looks enough like me to get away with fooling or there's a specific reason for what's going on and we need to find it. I know people who look alike yet when you get closer to them the difference would stand out like flashing neon lights."

Allen, one of the police forensic investigators, offered to make some prints we could take with us. "It'll only take a few minutes. Everything's digital these days." Before he handed them to me, he held them up one at a time. "I think you're mirror images of one another. It's a trait of identical twins. Her eyes are the same color as yours, as is her hair. The only thing I see to distinguish you is you're right-handed and the tapes indicate she's left-handed, which only strengthens the theory. Miss Nash, I'd say you have a twin— an identical twin."

The blood must have drained from my head. The room went in and out of focus. I grabbed on to Ryan to keep myself upright. I'd hoped the tapes would be proof she was an imposter, but it didn't happen. As impossible and implausible as it was, I was asked to accept the murder suspect as my twin sister. I didn't care what he thought he proved I knew I was an only child. It was too far-fetched to be true.

Roger came in. "I've been thinking. It might be a good idea to bring this out into the public eye. Put a picture of you and her in the local newspapers. Make it about doppelgangers. Everyone loves a good mystery. Someone might know this woman and give us a lead.

I handed the pictures to Ryan. "This is the same girl you think is on the run from the mob? Have you thought about the fact they could take me instead? I doubt it would do me any good to show them I'm right-handed so they'd know they didn't have the correct person."

I did my best not to dwell on it.

CHAPTER 8

I hadn't spent any time with Ryan since he came back from his business trip. It's true he stayed at the apartment and we had sex, but what we needed was a good old-fashioned date.

I called him. "Hi, are you busy tonight? I thought I'd make dinner. We could get a Red Box movie and spend some quality time together."

It sounded like he was driving with his window down because when he answered, I could hardly hear him. "Give me a minute," is what I thought I heard. I held the phone and waited. "Did I hear you ask me on a date?" He sounded like he was trying to stifle a laugh.

"Yes, you did. I think we could use some quiet time. I can cook."

"I didn't think you liked to cook. Tell you what. Let's cook together. I can get groceries on my way over."

"No, Ryan, I'll get groceries. I'm craving pasta with clams in white sauce. You get a movie and some ice cream from Ted Drew's. I'll take care of everything else."

"Okay, what time?" It was still difficult to hear him.

"Well." I looked at my cell phone. "It's five-thirty now, so whenever you can get here."

"Okay, see you in about an hour." He disconnected.

I smiled as I pulled into Schnuck's parking lot. If I had to go to pick up food, this was my store of choice. It had everything. I realized I was humming as I put my groceries in the cart.

"Hey, hey, Sophie." Some woman tapped me on the back. "Hey, Sophie, it's me, Janie. I didn't know you were back in St. Louis."

When I turned around, a woman, fortyish, in skin-tight leggings, a tank top three sizes too small, and over-dyed jet black hair, stood before me. She had a piece of gum in her mouth. It popped every time she chomped on it. She stood patiently—I guessed she expected an answer.

"I think you have me confused with someone else. My name isn't Sophie. I'm Kate Nash."

She had me pinned between the meat counter and her cart. "Okay, honey, be that way. I thought we were friends after all I did to help you." She leaned forward, looked around like she was afraid someone would overhear her. "Fine, I knew that story you told me was too strange to be real. And to think, all this time I have worried about your well-being. No more. You're on your own." She turned on her heel and thundered away. During the entire spiel, she never lost the rhythm as she chewed and popped.

I hesitated a moment too long. My brain engaged too late, I couldn't find her. I abandoned the shopping cart and ran down the aisles. When I was sure she wasn't in the store, I headed for the parking lot. No sign of her. *Sophie.* I guessed my criminal supposed to be twin's name was Sophie.

I found my cart once again and finished shopping. I went back for an extra bottle of Chardonnay.

Before Ryan arrived, I took a quick shower, changed into my favorite old jeans and a Cardinal tee shirt, popped the cork on a wine bottle, sat on the couch, sipped my drink, and pondered the encounter in the grocery store.

I didn't have much time to think before Ryan buzzed the intercom. Within moments, the room was full of life. Chili ran around yapping at him with her tail going ninety miles an hour. He reached down and picked her up. She licked his face, he rubbed her ears. It was fun to watch. I decided to put the Sophie incident on the back burner until after dinner.

"So does Chili get all the loving or do I get a hello kiss too?"

He leaned down and gave me a peck on the cheek and continued on to the kitchen with the dog in one hand and the bag he brought in with him in the other.

He sat the sack on the counter and gave all of his attention to Chili. "My, my, hasn't Kate been paying any attention to you?" He acted as if the dog talked back to him. "Really? She hasn't fed you in days? Here, let me fix that!" He reached into the bag and retrieved a fancy dog treat, sat Chili on the floor, and handed it to her. She ran to her bed by the terrace door and devoured it.

Ryan turned his attention to me. "How about a proper greeting? You look comfy."

"Are you disappointed I don't have anything sexy on?"

"Heavens no, I meant you really look comfy and I love it and you," he smiled.

"Well, thank you, Mr. Meade. You look pretty—well dressed-down—is the best I can come up with." I had yet to say those other three words back to him.

He gave me a hearty belly laugh and looked down at his jeans. They were tattered and faded in all the right places.

For the next hour we drank wine and kibitzed about his business trip as we cooked. By the time we had dinner on the table, we were relaxed and as happy as we had been in a while.

The pasta tasted amazing; hot, gooey buttery white sauce, shitake mushrooms, and clams over penne and a fresh garden salad on the side. We opened the second bottle of wine.

I hesitated to mention the incident in the grocery store and ruin the mood. I took a deep breath and began. "A lady, and I use the term loosely, came up to me at Schnucks. She mistook me for an old friend named Sophie. We stood nose to nose. If I appeared different, she didn't see it."

Ryan put his glass down and leaned in. "Did you ask her anything?"

I took a sip of wine. "No, I didn't put two and two together until she had moved on. I hunted all over the store, she was nowhere in sight. I ran around the parking lot. I exhausted all possibilities, gave up and went back to my shopping cart."

He reached over and touched my arm. "Don't be too upset. If it happened once, it'll happen again. I brought a good movie I've wanted to see."

I smiled and finished my dinner.

"Come here." He walked to my side of the table, reached down and lifted me to him. "Look at it this way. We know more than we did. We know she doesn't live in St. Louis, but she's here now, her name might be Sophie, and we know she's beautiful." He kissed me.

CHAPTER 9

A wet tongue in my ear woke me. Chili wanted to go outside. She was so short I had doggy steps against the bottom of the bed for her to use to get up and down. Ryan rolled my way. He must have gotten the same treatment.

He laughed and patted her head. "So much for a leisurely morning in bed." He was up and had his jeans on by the time I put my feet on the floor.

"You don't have to take her out."

"I love it. It's a beautiful morning. Want to go with us?"

I looked down at my shorts and oversized tee shirt and laughed. "No, not this time." I knew Chili couldn't hold it for as long as it would take for me to get ready.

He brought the newspaper back and sat at the table with his coffee. I fed the dog.

"What would you like to do today?"

"I hadn't thought about it." I had only thought about Sophie.

He kept reading. "I was hoping today would be the day you would move in with me."

I walked over, stood behind him, put my hands on his shoulders, and rubbed them. "Silly aren't I? I have no reason not to move ahead with you. We never fight. You're a wonderful man. Michael has been dead five years, so what stops me?"

He answered but didn't get up or turn around. "I know you love me, even though you don't say it. I know you love to have me around. So let's do it. If you don't like it you can come back here."

"I don't want to live in the mansion. Even though you have your living quarters warm and inviting, I couldn't call it home."

"I don't want to fight Michael's memories here anymore. Some of his clothes are still in the closet and his picture is in every room. I understand. He was one of my best friends. I don't expect you to forget him. Let's move to a neutral place that's never been yours or mine. Chili needs a yard and we should have a deck or patio so we can cook outdoors and look at the stars. What do you say?"

"I say yes. I swear I didn't know I would say yes. I thought I would say no. I don't think I have a grip on my emotions right now." I tingled.

The next couple of hours we listed features of the perfect home for us. We agreed on four bedrooms, three baths, a dead end street, a good neighborhood, and a basement to hide from the horrible storms St Louis was known for.

"What will you do with my apartment?"

"I bought the building several years ago so I think I'll keep it like it is for a while in case you want to come home once in a while. When you are certain you want to stay with me, I'll rent it out."

After we compiled a longer more detailed list, we showered and headed out to go house hunting.

We ate at a small outdoor café on the Loop, walked around the area and looked at the homes. Ryan waved his arms to encircle the area we were in. "How about living here?"

We stood in front of a two-story brick home with a huge yard and a privacy fence in the backyard. "It's kind of far from home," I joked.

"Come on, it's an open house, let's go in." He headed in that direction without waiting for my answer.

It fit our list perfectly, four bedrooms, four baths, living room, great room, sunroom off the kitchen and a patio with an outdoor kitchen. It had more features than our list. We both loved it.

"Let's make an offer." Ryan sounded pumped.

"Shouldn't we look at others so we can compare? No one buys the first house they see."

He put his arms out and turned around twice, much like Julie Andrews in the *Sound of Music*. "And why not? It has everything we want and more. Why waste time? From here, we can walk to our favorite places for coffee, dinner, a movie, and shopping. Chili will be safe in the yard and the house is a one-of-a-kind. I'll install a first-class security system in case one of the people you pick as a client wants to hurt you. I will rig the fence to protect Chili.

My nerves betrayed me. He turned me square to him. "Kate, it's a new beginning. Our lives will change for the better. It'll work out. If it doesn't, I'll move back to the Meade Estate."

"What do you mean *you will move?*"

"Well, since you're giving up your apartment, if we don't make it, this will be yours, or the Penthouse, your choice." He made a sweeping arc with his arm.

I couldn't think of anything to say. I was overwhelmed. When I settled down, I realized he was being Ryan. And Ryan loved me.

We were on a high as we walked around the block to explore our new neighborhood.

Sirens wailed. We looked at one another. It wasn't a high crime area. The sound grew to an ear-bursting level as they roared our way from both directions.

Someone yelled through a bullhorn. "Get on your knees. Put your hands on your head." We glanced around to see who they were talking to. Several armed officers exited the cars, guns drawn, and ran toward us.

I couldn't follow or hear his directions due to the noise. Before I could object, I was on the ground on my stomach with my hands behind my back. A cop sat on me as he put handcuffs on my wrists. I looked up. Ryan had gotten the same treatment. Two officers bound his wrists.

"What's going on here?" Ryan tried to raise his head off the concrete sidewalk.

"I'll ask the questions." The cop had his hand on the back of Ryan's collar.

He let go. Ryan's head bounced twice. Blood oozed from his cheek.

I'd been mistaken for Sophie. Wait until they found out they had Ryan Meade in handcuffs. This would not be good.

We lay as we were for about ten minutes. No one talked to us or looked in our direction. A young man walked up to Ryan. "Sorry, boss. I tried to tell them who you are, but no one's listening. The other woman; the one who looks like your lady, was seen around here again. You know they have a warrant out for her because she's a suspect in a murder investigation?"

"You tried to tell them, Ethan. I'm sure you did your best."

Ethan was one of Ryan's security men. I knew some of them were police officers who supplemented their income with an extra job. I didn't know which ones.

"Yes, I did. That's why we're standing around. They don't want to let her go if she's the perp and they don't know what to do about you. We're waiting for a guy from downtown named Roger Simon.
He's at a christening and we can't get to him for another fifteen minutes or so."

"Can we at least sit up?" Ryan looked my way.

Ethan walked off and called back over his shoulder. "Let me go see what I can do."

Another minute or two passed and two patrol officers came over and helped Ryan to sit. They did the same for me. Blood trickled down Ryan's face.

What a mess.

We were a curiosity. People from all over the neighborhood had come out of their homes and speculated about what we might have done. Of course, the news outlets followed the police scanners. Cameras clicked in every direction.

We waited, not too patiently.

I got Ryan's attention. "Do you think Ethan would call Amy? Chili's been alone a long time and I don't see this situation coming to a resolution any time soon."

He whistled and Ethan turned around. The young man made the call. I relaxed a little.

The concrete was cold, damp, and hard. For over two hours we sat there. Roger was nowhere in sight. The folks in the neighborhood lost interest. Two men watched us. The rest of them left the scene.

Roger arrived in a worse mood than we were. "Kate. Ryan." He curtly nodded to each of us in turn. "Take those handcuffs off these people and let them go." The two cops looked at one another, looked around the area. No one was there to tell them what to do. Roger kept his composure and told them again to let us go.

The older cop nodded toward me. "But, sir, the lady is wanted for murder."

"I know it's confusing, but trust me, you need to let them go. This gentleman is Ryan Meade and I assure you they did nothing wrong." The color of Roger's face and his clenched fists convinced them to listen. I was intimidated and I was innocent.

The young officer didn't move a muscle. "I need to check on this, sir."

Roger put his hands on his hips. "You do that, officer. We'll wait."

In a minute he came back, helped us to our feet, removed the handcuffs, and left the scene.

Roger walked toward the street. We fell into step next to him. "I think it's time to take this seriously."

Ryan stepped closer to me and put his hand on my elbow to escort me. I took a tissue out of my pocket and handed it to him to wipe, the now dried, blood off his cheek.

Roger turned and looked me in the eye. "Are you taking this seriously? Maybe she didn't kill that man, but we won't know if she doesn't come in. Nobody goes to that much trouble to become a double and runs away. I'm not sure how, but you two are related. I watched her move in those videos. It was you, Kate. I worked with you for years and I can't tell the difference. I'd follow that path and see where it leads you."

Roger drove us back to the Loop.

Ryan walked toward Starbucks. "Got time for a cup of coffee, Roger?"

"Sure, why not?"

Roger had his cup to his lips but didn't take a sip. "I don't get it, Kate."

"What don't you get?" Everyone in the coffee shop stared at me. My face was on every television screen in the St. Louis metro area and that covered a massive amount of territory and included part of Illinois.

Roger shook his head. "We have a woman who looks like you, dresses like you, and drives an old BMW, like you. Why?"

Ryan patted my hand. "Good questions."

I reached into my jacket pocket and took out my notepad. "I've been going over the reasons people are victims of identity theft. None of them comes close to what's happening here. This is personal. She may not be running. I can't get my mind around it. In my entire life, I have never seen anyone who resembles me. I don't look like my mother." I knew I sounded depressed, but I couldn't help it.

"Could you have a twin you don't know about? A child your mother gave away or something?"

I looked from one of them to the other. "My mom would never do anything like that."

"Well, I say you ask her, just in case." Roger was serious.

"That's ridiculous." I tried to smile.

Roger stared at me. "Is it?"

"Here's what we know so far." Roger made his case. He touched each finger as if to keep track. "The car was between a 1980 and '84 BMW. My guys found it in a parking garage on the east side. Someone stole everything out of it that was worth anything. There were no fingerprints or licenses plates. We got the serial number off it and it has a salvage title from Florida. It is registered to a T. Bell, last known address, 1000 Disney Way, Orlando. The films we have of her show she's left-handed, and someone has a healthy sense of humor. Other than that, there are no differences between you.

"I've been reading about identical twins and in most cases they're mirror images of one another, so since you are right handed, it makes sense. I've watched the surveillance tapes about a hundred times. Whoever she is, on the first tape it looks like she shot someone. Once we had them enhanced and studied them from every direction, she looks terrified of something just out of camera range, behind her. She looks back when she hears the first shot. It looks like she's clinging to a piece of jewelry, not a gun. It's too small to be the kind of weapon used to shoot him. Our investigation shows the bullets came from a further distance and the angle makes the CSI team believe they came from somewhere up higher. There are four tall buildings around there. The men are searching for clues."

I sat looking at my hands. "I read about identical twins also. You're right. She and I fit all of the common traits. If you take a good look at her, she even has the same style slacks as I do." I tried to keep my voice steady and strong, but I was unnerved and Ryan must have picked up on it.

He stood. "Let's get you home."

We thanked Roger for his help. Ryan ushered me out of the store and into the truck. I didn't feel safe until I was in my apartment and the elevator door had closed behind me.

CHAPTER 10

We sat in the living room and watched the news. I was the feature story. *St.Louis's own Kate Nash who can forget the triple homicide her agency solved a couple of years ago?—seems to have a look-a-like. They're known as doppelgangers. Doppelganger, for those of you who aren't familiar with the term, is someone who looks like you but isn't you. Sounds like science fiction doesn't it? We have Dr. Sara Dancing in the studio with us. Dr. Dancing is a professor of paranormal studies at one of our leading universities.*

The good doctor spent five minutes showing pictures of look-alikes and sharing facts about these paranormal pairs. Paranormal entities rarely did anything on their own and out of character for the clone she represented. *Most of them were seen out of the corner of the eye or stood behind the person as they looked in the mirror. On the other hand, Catherine the Great walked into the throne room one day and stood face to face with her doppelganger as it sat casually on the throne.*

The night Lincoln became our President, he happened to catch a glimpse of himself in a mirror, but two honest Abes stared back at him.

She went on and I had to admit, it held my interest. I didn't believe it and I could tell Ryan didn't either. There had to be a real, solid, human out there who came to St. Louis and looked like me.

Ryan picked up the TV remote and pressed the mute button. "So much for not alerting the De Marcos there are two of you. Hopefully, gangsters don't watch TV. Tell me again about your father."

I acted like I didn't hear him. It didn't deter him. "Tell me about your father?"

"There isn't much to tell. He died before I was born. He stepped on a landmine in the Persian Gulf. Mom never married again."

He took a pad out of his jacket pocket and took notes. "Where was your dad from?"

"Round Rock, Texas, I've racked my brain and I can't think of how this all fits together. We need to come up with some kind of plan to find Sophie."

"Only a couple of things can be happening here. Either she had plastic surgery or you indeed have a twin." He turned to me. "Did you hear the name of the college where Dr. Dancing worked?"

"No. It was that old *leading university* thing." I couldn't keep the irritation out of my voice.

"We need to track her down or hire our own expert and find out what's true and what isn't about doppelgangers. This is the thing of movies and television. It seems farfetched to me."

I had to agree. "I don't need to know anything more about them. According to what I have heard all of my life, if she is my twin, I will be able to sense it when I see her face to face."

We sat in silence and watched the rest of the news. It featured a tape of us as we sat cross-legged on the sidewalk in University City with our hands cuffed behind our backs. It wasn't a pretty picture. I wanted a hot shower, a good meal, and for the day to fade away.

I hugged Chili tighter. What did I do before I had her?

I changed the subject. "I have a case in St. Charles tomorrow. A woman is trying to get custody of her children. She's using the fact that their father has numerous women in the house at all hours. She needs proof to have him declared an unfit parent. I'm meeting Amy at five a.m. at the Starbucks on Fifth Street. We'll plan our strategy."

He gave me a look I couldn't read. "You can't work a case. You sitting in a car outside a house could get you killed. People are afraid of you Kate. It'd be best if you stayed in and out of sight until we find Sophie."

My eyes filled with tears. Jeez. I hated to cry. I turned my head away and was saved when my cell phone rang. I reached down to pick it up. The caller ID read *restricted number.* My stomach churned.

Now what? I turned the phone toward Ryan so he could read the screen before I answered it. "Kate Nash here."

"I'm sorry about today, and last week and, well, all of it. If I could stop it I would."

I pushed the button to turn on the speaker. Her voice was soft and her speech patterns halting as if she was uncertain what she wanted to say. She spoke with a heavy Eastern accent. "Who is this?"

"I'm sure I'm your sister. I can't talk now. They're following me. I didn't want to bring you into this, so stay home for a few days until I can get out of here."

"Tell me what's going on. Who wants to harm you? Why would someone try to make it seem like you're a criminal; like *I* am a criminal?"

"I saw your picture in the paper after your artist friend was found. I wanted to come to St. Louis and see you, perhaps talk. It seems my *family* obligations are getting in the way." She sounded tired and beaten. "I'm going to go home. It's the only thing that will stop all of this. In a few weeks,

I'll contact you and maybe we can meet. I'm truly sorry for the trouble this has caused you. If I stay here, things will only get worse."

"Sophie, you can't leave now. Let's clear your name and confront your family. Whatever it is, I'm sure we can fix it." I tried not to sound desperate. She seemed so sure, I needed to know what she knew that I didn't. I'd gone over it a million times and it wasn't possible.

"If by *clear my name*, you mean the man who was shot in front of me. I didn't do that. It was a man my father sent to take me home. I'm sure a rival *family* shot him. I do know it saved me from being dragged home by the hair. I'm sorry, perhaps another time and place. I'm not trying to keep secrets. The more you know, the more danger you could be in. My family can be very unforgiving." She hung up.

I turned to Ryan. "Did you hear what she said?"

"I did."

I put my phone in my pocket and sat next to him on the couch. "What do you think?"

"That she's either guessing because you look so much like her or that she found out an old family secret and used it to find you. Come here."

He put his arms out and I slipped into them. "It's not something I'm able to come to terms with. If I do it means I have to suspend what I know to be the truth of my childhood."

Ryan hugged a little tighter. I laid my head on his chest and tried to forget what I'd heard and relaxed a little. The force with which my heart beat against my chest, made it impossible.

CHAPTER 11

A t eight the next morning, the phone rang. I sat on the balcony with a cup of latte to enjoy the cool weather. Chili slept on my lap under a throw I had on my knees. Ryan was in the shower.

"This is Roger. Seems there was an incident with your friend. Witnesses saw her being chased. She looked back over her shoulder, knocked over an elderly couple and ran off through the Art Museum parking lot. She got into an older model dark green Impala and drove away. On the way out, she sideswiped a car. The men who were on her heels were arrested and detained by the Park Police. They're transferring them over here. I expect them in about an hour. Would you like to come listen in?"

While he talked, I went into the house. "I don't get it. At first, it looked as if she killed a man, then it turned out she didn't have a gun but took the time to take some piece of jewelry out of his pocket, and the dead man was mixed up with the Mafia. The woman in the grocery store specifically called her *Sophie*. Now, more men chased her."

Roger used his professional voice. "Are you coming to listen in or not? And how do you know her name is Sophie?"

"It's the name the lady in the store called me when she thought I was her friend from some years ago. Last night Sophie called here. I used the name Sophie and she didn't correct me. I'll tell you about it when I see you."

Ryan came into the kitchen to get coffee. He was dressed in dark slacks, a pale pink Polo shirt and a dark maroon sports coat. "Don't you look spiffy?" I walked over and kissed him. "Roger called. There was an incident at the Art Museum this morning. Two men chased Sophie. The Park Police caught and arrested them. Roger invited me to come down to Central to listen while he interviews them. Do you have time to go?"

"Sure." He headed toward the couch. "Are you going like that?"

I took a quick shower and dressed more formally than usual because Ryan looked so polished.

Nothing had changed at the Central Police Station since I worked there years ago. The noise level made you wish you had earplugs. There was a flow, but if you weren't privy to it, you would think the place was a refereed free-for-all. An officer let us into one of the observation rooms with a two-way mirror.

Roger sat in a sparsely decorated room on the other side. A well-dressed man in his forties sat across the table from him. I had been at the same table with hundreds of criminals and this man didn't look like one. He was dressed as if he belonged in an office building or in a courtroom to defend a client.

The officer flipped a switch and sound flowed clearly out of two speakers on the wall. Roger had a legal pad in front of him. "Who was the lady you were chasing and why were you chasing her?"

The man reached for the cuff on his right shirt sleeve and pulled it down until a cufflink came into view. He did the same on the left side and rested both arms on the table. "I

didn't chase anyone. The lady was ahead of me in line waiting for the place to open. She looked at me and I thought she
was going to faint. She screamed and ran out. Since I was the
one who scared her naturally I ran out to see if I could help
her."

"Naturally." Roger held up the suspect's driver's license. "It says here you're from Newark, New Jersey. Is that
correct?"

"That is correct. Unless the law has changed, it's not
against the law to live in Jersey. He pronounced it *Jouysee.*

Roger tossed the man's wallet across the table. "Show
me a permit for the .357 the officers took from you."

"Sure." He leafed through the cards in his billfold,
picked one out and slid it across the table. "I got it right
here."

The door opened. An officer stuck his head in. "Mr. Sabatini's lawyer has arrived."

Roger shook his head. "Show him in."

The man who walked into the room was even better
dressed than the man already seated. He offered Roger a card
and a handshake. "I'm Anthony Patroni. I represent Dominic
De Marco and his business enterprises." He looked away
from Roger and spoke to the prisoner. "Where's Tony?"

"I haven't seen him since we got here," he answered.

The high priced attorney addressed Roger. "I would ap-
preciate it if Mr. Romo was allowed to join us. I read the report on the way in and I know you have to let these men go.
I'd rather have them together so we can cut down the time by
handling both men at once."

Roger looked down at the card in his hand as if he
couldn't remember the attorney's name. "Take a seat, Mr.
Patroni. We don't always get what we want at the time we
want it. There are a few things I'd like to clear up before we
discuss the men's release." Roger pushed a button and the
door opened again and who I guessed to be Tony Romo
came in and sat in a chair near the table.

Ryan and I looked at one another.

If the lawyer was upset, he didn't show it. He sat straight in his seat and never took his gaze off Roger. "What would you like to know?"

The attorney acknowledged the new man in the room. "Good to see you, Romo."

Roger waited until the man was settled. "What kind of business would take Mr. De Marco's employees to the Art Museum at seven o'clock on a Tuesday morning?"

The older man nodded to the two, indicating they should answer the question.

Romo spoke up. "There's a Norman Rockwell exhibition, and we both read *The Saturday Evening Post* when we were kids. We wanted to see it. So did everyone else in St. Louis. We arrived at seven and there were already at least a hundred people in line."

Roger persisted. "Funny, you don't look that old. Mr. Rockwell died in 1978. Did you know the lady you went to help?"

"No," Sam Sabatini joked. "We're just nice guys that way."

Ryan and I were still seated on the other side of the two-way mirror. We could hear every word, and at that moment you could have heard a pin drop.

This was better than any movie I'd seen in the recent past.

The attorney smiled and showed a mouth full of ultra white teeth. "We don't get into what the men do in their free time."

"Your boss' men were seen chasing a woman this morning in Forest Park. We don't like it when people are chased for no reason."

He looked around the little room as though someone might be hidden in it. "I'm sure Sam and his co-worker, Mr. Romo both gave you a good reason for their actions."

"These men ran through a very populated area of the Park, an elderly couple were knocked down, and injured. It's unacceptable behavior in our city." I thought Roger wanted to anger the lawyer.

Anthony Patroni reached into his inside jacket pocket and pulled out a checkbook. "Since no one has filed a complaint against these men and they have the proper paperwork for their weapons. I want them released immediately and their weapons returned to them. Mr. De Marco would be distressed if he knew anyone was injured in this mishap. Here's a check made out to cash, tell the couple how sorry the men are. Have them use this money for any expenses they might encounter." When he laid it down, I saw his manicured fingernails.

Roger picked the check up off the table and took a step so he was between the door and the men. "This is extremely generous of Mr. De Marco, but we cannot accept any money from you."

"I assure you, detective. It's legal."

All three men walked out. I knew there was nothing more Roger could do. Without Sophie to explain why she was frightened enough to run blindly and leave in such a hurry she side-swiped another car, there was no case.

Roger came out of the interrogation room and into the other side where we sat. "What do you two make of that?"

I gave my opinion first. "I think whoever Sophie is, she's afraid of the De Marcos. I think it would be a bad idea, from what we heard, to put any kind of article or pictures in the newspapers. I'm not sure what trouble the news report on television will stir up. We could cause her and me a lot of trouble. Now's not the time for anyone else to find out there are two of us; if they don't know already."

Roger sat on the edge of the table. "I agree. You two need to stay here until those men are processed and released. We don't want them to see you."

Ryan remained seated and wrote more notes on his notepad. "I think we need to find out all we can about the *De Marco Family*. I say, family, because I know a little bit about them. The name has come up several times when we try to

branch out in the Northeast. One of their operations sells protection. No one up in that area wants their business to have
alarms and cameras. I think I understand why."

CHAPTER 12

The alarm sounded at four a.m. I jumped as if I'd heard a gunshot. Ryan stirred beside me. Chili snuggled farther under the covers between us. I knew it was now or never. I hustled into the bathroom and turned the shower on as hot as I could stand it. I always considered the little pleasures to be big blessings; hot water, fresh coffee, clean sheets, and soft towels, were a few.

It was the first time I woke in the morning with Ryan and didn't think about Michael. Maybe I had finally found a place to tuck him in my heart from time to time.

Before I dressed, I called Amy to make sure she was awake. The key to a successful surveillance was to set up early so you looked like you belonged in the neighborhood as to not arouse suspicion.

She answered on the first ring. I found her annoyingly happy in the morning.

When I stepped out of the closet fully dressed, Ryan sat up on the side of the bed. "My goodness, you're moving fast today. And you look gorgeous."

I blushed, walked up to him and stood as close as I could. "You look pretty good yourself."

"I see I didn't talk you out of taking the St. Charles case. At least let me go along to keep you safe."

I kissed him. "Ryan, I know you're looking out for me, but Amy and I can handle this. Besides, she doesn't like it when you and I work together. She feels expendable and I can't have that."

He didn't say anything for a moment. He pulled me to him and hugged me tightly. "I can't let anything happen to you. Be careful, just because Sophie intends to leave doesn't mean you won't get mistaken for her. Do or say what you want, but I'll be there or one of my men will."

I opened my mouth to object. He placed his finger lightly on my lips and stopped me before he continued. "You won't know we're there. We're professionals."

He wasn't about to back down so I agreed. I didn't want to admit it but I already relaxed and some of the angst left my body.

Amy sat at a small table in the back of the coffee shop. She looked amazing, tall and straight. She could wear anything and flaunted it with wild colors and the latest fashion trends. She had dozens of pairs of half glasses in all colors and styles. She picked a pair to accent her outfit and hung them around her neck on a silver chain. She looked over the top of them when she had something to say.

Today she had no makeup, a simple black sweater and skin-tight black jeans. Her long legs stuck out from under the table. Her hair lay nicely around her face without the usual bows and bobbles.

She waved at me and pushed a cup of latte and a bagel to my side of the table. "You're right on time. Cohabitating seems to agree with you."

My face got hot. "It does. You look wonderful. Are you ready for this great adventure?"

She put her hand on mine and leaned forward. "Are you? No one's pretending to be me. I don't have to worry every minute about being shot or arrested for crimes I didn't commit."

"I have to. I can't let this rule my life." I filled her in on the conversation I'd had with Sophie on the phone the night before. Until we found out who she was, where she came from, and if she was my sister, I needed to try to maintain a normal life. I needed proof. To know it in my heart only convinced me, no one else. I heard the people at the next table talk about me. They speculated as to who I was.

Amy stood, picked up her coffee cup and headed toward the door. I followed suit. On the way out, I set my things on the young couple's tabletop, took one of my business cards from my back pocket, and laid it in front of the girl. I flashed my biggest smile at everyone in the place before I walked calmly out the door.

CHAPTER 13

I looked around for Ryan or his men. Even though I was certain they were there, I didn't see them. The case wouldn't take too long. Twenty minutes after his wife left for work, James Turner, returned to his house with a lady in a business suit. He couldn't keep his hands off her. They were inside about two hours. The only movement we could see came from an upstairs corner room. It was nothing blatant, but obviously a bedroom.

Amy took a dozen pictures of him and his woman as they walked to the house and several more when they left together in a blue Ford Escape. Within an hour, he came back. This time the female with him looked like a hooker. She had enough make up on for four women, and a red push up bra I didn't need the binoculars to see. It shoved her well endowed chest up so it hung out over her blouse.

If what happened in the house was as it appeared, then Mr. Turner was a scumbag.

We didn't see any movement upstairs. I got out of the car, sneaked around to the back and peeked in a window. I turned around to head back to the car and ran smack into my nemesis.

"Shush," she whispered. I obeyed, not because she scared me, but because I was shocked by her looks. Without a doubt, we were twins. No one was that good of a plastic surgeon. She took my hand and led me to a dark green Chevy Impala. It didn't have license plates.

She opened the door "Get in."

I lost my balance and fought to right myself. I heard someone behind me shout. "Stop! Put your hands up."

She jumped into the car on her side and sped off. I hung on half in the front seat and half out. I let go. The car dragged me about ten feet. My left leg and arm were in the car. She slowed down as she turned a corner at the end of an alley. My head bounced on the ground and hit a utility pole. Sticky liquid ran out of my forehead, and into my eyes.

Someone handed me a cloth. Nathan stood over me. He pressed as hard as he could on the wound. Amy ran toward us at breakneck speed; gun drawn. "What happened?"

"It was Sophie. She looked like me, down to the mole at my hairline." I knew I sounded alarmed and breathless. I'd seen her on television, but to have her next to me—was indescribable. "And the other strange thing, I knew her, like an old friend from childhood."

I looked away when I heard a car door. Ryan sprinted to my side. He didn't say a word. He took me in his arms and held me tight. I bled all over his clean white shirt.

Nathan broke the silence. "Our guys went after her. They lost her on Kings Highway. She turned left down a one way street and Dale got stuck behind a school bus full of children. He had to stop while they unloaded."

Ryan still didn't answer. He eased his hold and helped me stand.

"Amy, can you take Kate by the hospital, or urgent care and get her head looked at?"

"Sure."

I looked from him to Amy. "Ryan, I don't think I need stitches."

Simultaneously they answered. "Yes, you do."

It was a quiet ride to the emergency room. I tried to remember every detail of her face and her hair. However; it was more than that. I recognized her smell and the turn of her neck. I had a sister, a twin; identical. I'd never experienced anything compared to it. The other side of having a sister, much less a twin would have to include lies. Maybe I had been kidnapped at birth. There were infinite possibilities and none of them were good.

I wondered if she had the same sensation I as when we were in the same space at the same time.

I didn't have to wait for treatment. It seemed head wounds bled a lot. I was covered in blood, yet it took a scant two stitches to close the gash. My head throbbed. I heard the doctor tell Amy not to let me go to sleep for any length of time. She agreed and they let us go.

I couldn't think of anything or anyone except Sophie. Life seemed different. Why hadn't she gone to my apartment and rang the bell? Why become a criminal to get my attention? She'd confessed it wasn't what it appeared. Then what was it? My head ached from the wound and the mystery.

I needed to talk to Mother.

Ryan was home when I arrived. He'd already figured out some answers. But at least part of them rested in Florida with Mom. He had his cell phone in his hand and laid it down as I walked over to him. "We have two tickets to St. Petersburg in the morning. I didn't think we should leave right now because of your head. You look exhausted."

"I am. I need to think. It was surreal. I don't know how this happened. I don't know why no one told me about her, but she's my sister, my twin. I'd bet my life on it. When I looked into her eyes, it was like looking in a mirror. When she realized you might catch her, she slowed down and pushed me out. Had she not, I'd have been seriously hurt."

Ryan helped me out of my bloody clothes as we talked. "I don't understand."

Amy had headed back to our surveillance with Nathan. They wanted to try to salvage the case. We'd created such a scene, I wasn't sure she could pull it off; maybe no one put it together.

Ryan tried to soothe me, but it did no good. My entire life had turned into a lie in the last few hours. It left me exhausted and confused.

I put on some loose clothes and lay down. I dropped into a deep fitful sleep filled with my mother, Sophie, and dead bodies. Every time something meaningful formed in my dream, Ryan's voice broke through and woke me, checked my pupils, and bugged me with questions like what year was it and who was the current President. My head wound would not allow me to come out of the fog. This must have gone on for hours, because when I got up at nine-thirty the next morning, I didn't feel like I had solved a thing.

By noon, we were at the airport. My wound throbbed. If I put my hand down I could feel my pulse pounding in my fingers. It was a strange sensation. I didn't want to talk or sleep. I wanted to look out the window and try to get my head around what had happened to my life.

I knew Mother held the answers.

CHAPTER 14

We landed in St. Petersburg around five-thirty and rented a car at the airport. Mom lived a short walk from St. Pete's beach in a condo she bought when I was in the third grade.

She sat in the shade on the back covered deck when we walked up. "My goodness, Katie, is everything alright? Goodness do you have a cut on your pretty face?"

"Yes, Mom, I'm fine. It's a small cut on my forehead. I need to talk to you about something and I needed to do it in person."

She acted like she noticed Ryan for the first time. Maybe she did. "Mr. Meade, so nice to see you again."

"Please, call me Ryan, Mrs. Madison."

She smiled. "You may call me Denise."

Anger welled up inside me. "Mom, we need to talk. Come inside."

"You're frightening me dear. Whatever's wrong?" She made no effort to move from her chair or put her magazine down. I thought it a strange reaction considering I'd flown over a thousand miles, unannounced. to see her.

"Now, Mother. We need to talk, now."

Ryan walked over and stood beside me. He put his hand on my shoulder. If it was supposed to settle me down it didn't work. I was much too upset.

I put both hands on my hips and glared at my mother until she moved. She knew why I was there, how could she not? She didn't live in a vacuum. She had a daughter who was the subject of the evening news, I knew for a fact it became a national story and Mother never missed the news. I had also told her some of the stories myself to minimize what she might have heard. I wanted answers.

She went through the motions of politeness and served us ice tea. If she didn't sit down soon I'd have to scream. "What is it dear?"

I looked at Ryan. He had an expression on his face I couldn't read. Perhaps he wanted to give me more time. "Denise, yesterday Kate came into direct contact with a woman she believes to be her sister; her twin sister. Can you explain that to us?"

My mother looked straight at me. If she was shocked by Ryan's statement, she didn't let on. "No. I don't believe I can."

"Why's that, Mom? If I have a sister I think you'd be the first to know."

She rubbed her hands down her legs as if to straighten an unseen wrinkle in her housedress. "It isn't possible. No. You cannot have a sister. It just isn't possible."

"Are *you* my mother?" I didn't care if it sounded cruel or not. I wanted the truth.

"I've always been your mother." For the first time since our arrival, her façade crumbled. She picked at her skirt and lowered her head.

My voice quivered. Had my entire life been a lie? "Let me rephrase my question. Did you give birth to me?"

My mother put her hands up to her face. I stood and walked over to stand in front of her. When she didn't look up, I knelt in front of her. "Mother, did you give birth to me or not?"

She wouldn't look at me. "No."

I took her hands in mine and tried to pull them away from her face. She would not allow it. I squeezed them the next time I tried. I wanted to see her face while she told me I no longer had an identity it had taken me over thirty years to create and get comfortable with. My voice choked. "Is John Madison my father?" I needed to move the conversation forward.

"No, I never met John Madison."

I sat down before I fainted. Ryan stood. I raised my hand and signaled *no* to him.

I needed a little time. I sat in the nearest chair and took a deep breath. In Yoga, they taught -step back and breathe. It seemed the most logical thing to do in the wake of finding out my entire life was a lie. I sat and tried to focus on my breathing.

It played like a scene in a movie. I heard Mom. She cried and took in choppy breaths; the wind chime tinkled in the breeze, along with the hum of the filter on the swimming pool, each of them became a distinct sound in the otherwise silent room.

The jingle of my cell phone pierced the quiet. I took it out of my pocket and looked at it. It flashed *restricted number*. I knew who it was. I showed it to Ryan as I brushed past him to take the call in private. "I'm glad you called, Sophie. I didn't think I would hear from you for awhile. Why do you always know where I am?"

I realized I had such a tight grip on the phone, my hand ached.

"That's a fair question. Did you look into the background of the men who tried to take me at the Art Museum?"

I turned around and looked through the door to see what Mother and Ryan were doing. They appeared to be deep in conversation. "I know they are Mafia from New Jersey.

When you speak of *your family* do you mean the De Marcos?"

"Yes, I'm Sophia De Marco, but history tells me he isn't our father."

"Who is he and why are you running from him?"

"Oh, Kate dear, I wish I had the time to tell you what I know. I feel like Cinderella. If I don't make it back before the end of the week, I may never get to leave again. Ask your mother who we are. She has more information than I. The extent of my knowledge is Dominic says he's my father but he isn't, and our mother is dead. Some say she died the night we were born; others say she was collateral damage in a mob shootout in New York City when I was eight.

"I also know whatever reason they had to separate us at birth doesn't matter anymore, but it went on so long they didn't know what to do."

"This is so sordid. Why didn't they let us know about one other when it no longer mattered?"

"Kate, you can't undo a nearly thirty-five-year lie without destroying the world."

"They *have* destroyed *my* life."

"And mine." She hung up.

I had more questions than ever. I wondered about the woman I'd known all my life. My legs weakened and my head ached. As I opened the door I noticed Ryan had a cloth in his hand. Mother looked faint.

Before Sophie came into my life, my mom was the best mom in the world. She had always been there for me, gave love and understanding at every point of my life. I reminded myself she was still the same woman. I didn't want to destroy our bond. My thought boomeranged and slammed me in the face. We had no bond. Our relationship had been built on a lie. I wanted to believe her every action was meant to protect me from something or someone. But I had to know.

I knelt in front of her again. She looked up, straight into my eyes. "I'm so sorry I didn't tell you. Back then I couldn't tell you for fear they would come take you away from me. You have had my heart since you were a few hours old."

"Mother, where did you get me?" I wanted to sit, yet I wanted to hold her hands to make sure I could see her eyes- and detect a lie. I didn't know how I could have lived my life to adulthood and never know about my past.

What child doubts their mother about the circumstances of their birth?

"Kate, I've been going to tell you many times but each time fear took the lead and I couldn't"

"Couldn't what, Mom? What's so scary you were too afraid to talk?" I tried to remain patient. "I won't let anyone hurt you. I'm almost thirty-five years old. No one can come and take me now."

Mom looked at Ryan and back to me. "Sit down, honey and I'll tell you the entire story. But I must tell you right now, it doesn't involve a sister for you, much less a twin sister."

I moved over and sat on the couch next to Ryan. He took my hand.

"Have you ever heard the name, Maroni Lombardi?"

"He was the last of the New York crime bosses to be gunned down in a Mafia war. In the late fifties, I believe," Ryan answered. "What does he have to do with this?"

"Everything, he had a daughter, Julia Lombardi. She got pregnant by a member of another crime family. Before she could deliver the child, she was killed in an automobile accident. They saved the baby. You're that baby."

I felt faint. Ryan let go of my hand and drew me towards him, he bore the brunt of my weight. "So who was John Madison? You said earlier you never met him. So my father's a lie also?"

"I didn't know anyone named John Madison. The picture is that of a boyfriend of a girl I knew in St. Louis. He was killed in action and I needed a father figure for you. Someone you could look up to. Besides, I couldn't have a baby out of wedlock and still be respectable."

"I find that hard to believe. I was born in 1980. It wasn't the dark ages. Plenty of women had babies."

"It wasn't the life for me, dear. I was twenty-nine. I had never been married. I had a successful career as a surgical nurse. All I had to do to have the child I always wanted was to make up a dead husband, move out of St. Louis to a spot where no one knew me and build a new life. You were my reward."

"Do you hear what you're saying? I was a reward like a teddy bear you win for knocking down the milk bottles at a carnival. What about Sophie? If there were two babies, why didn't you take both? If you were there, you would have to know the woman had twins." I wanted the entire story. "If you were afraid they would take me back, there must have been more to it."

"I got a phone call about nine o'clock on the day you were born. Dr. Signorelli wanted me to come to the hospital. Honor Hospital was known as the *Mafia Hospital*. It was a privately owned entity where some not so law abiding citizens came with injuries, and for plastic surgery, among other things. "Men who were killed were sometimes brought there to make them look better before their families saw them. Let's just say I helped the *family* in times of difficulty."

I pressed her for more. "What kinds of *difficulty*?"

She glanced at Ryan. I think she needed to find an ally. "I don't see how any of the details will help you find out who this Sophie person is or help you in any way."

"Indulge me, Mother."

She stopped, took the cloth she had been using to blot her face, and put it on the table next to her. "I am done for now. This subject has given me a raging migraine and I must lie down. We'll talk more after dinner. Ryan, could you handle dinner plans, dear?"

She was gone. I stared after her. She didn't seem to be intimidated by me or my questions. This person was a stranger to me.

I went to the room Ryan and I shared and laid my suitcase on the bed. He followed me. "I'm going down to the beach to find a nice place for dinner. I won't be gone long."

I fell into a fitful sleep full of people who looked like me. They were ahead of me in line at the grocery store, at the post office, the doctor's office; the toll collector on the bridge was my double as was the waiter, and the car wash attendant. When I dragged myself back to the present, my mother sat across from me. "You know I regret this, right, Kathleen?"

"Regret what, Mom, lying to me for all these years about a father who never even existed? What about all those stories you told me about my so-called paternal grandparents? Or the long labor you had when you gave birth to me. It's been nothing but lies since I was born."

I quit because the tears streamed down my mom's face. As mad as I was at that moment, I didn't have it in me to be mean to her.

Ryan danced into the room. I knew he hadn't expected my mom to be there. He held a bouquet of flowers in his hand, sported a St. Pete's Beach Sand Volleyball cap, and carried a bag in his other hand. "I made reservations at Woody's Waterfront Café for seven. I thought we needed a little diversion." His gaze bounced from Mom to me. "I want to remind you two that when this is all out in the open, you'll still love each other deeply and everything will be fine."

I watched as mom gave him a weak smile. I looked at him with disdain.

I glanced at the clock on the wall near the closet. We needed to leave for the restaurant. Apparently, we would leave the family drama for a later time. I didn't know for sure how I felt about it. Mom and Ryan seemed pleased.

We walked down the beach to the café. It was a beautiful evening. The tide was out. Every light on land reflected perfectly back across the water. It calmed my soul. I knew this was a much-needed break from the story unfolding. I went with the flow.

Mom and I ordered margaritas and Ryan ordered a beer. We had smoked fish dip, talked about the weather, our surroundings, but not much else. Dinner tasted amazing and the walk back to Mom's condo gave me the perspective I needed to put it all in its place. I had a good childhood. Every night I went to bed smiling, warm, and well fed. Maybe mother had a good reason for what she had done. But my sixth sense told me it was all a lie. My brain needed some time to process what I heard earlier.

It was hard to get my head around the fact that I was the daughter of a *mafia mol*.

Mother promised to tell us the rest of her story the next morning. She looked tired and aged. I'd never thought of her as old before. Her posture had always been ramrod straight. She was taller than me. Her chin remained chiseled and her arms didn't sag. She did Yoga three days a week, swam daily and planned to teach math at the local elementary school for several more years.

To teach in Florida she had to be bilingual. She switched from English to Spanish at will.

No matter what she did, I knew I couldn't discount what she had done for me all my life. I didn't believe it, yet I held out hope.

When we got back to the house, Mother excused herself and went to her room. Ryan and I ditched our shoes and walked on the beach. The moon hung like an orange balloon in the sky. As the waves lapped the shore, the light traveled on the surface of the ocean. We stood in silence and watched it. The moon shined on the water at the horizon and its light traveled to us on the water with every wave. We walked a long time in silence.

The ocean renewed me. As a child I sat on the same beach and made up stories about what happened under the water. Once I fabricated a story so scary I didn't get in the water for the entire summer.

For the first time, I questioned where the money had come from. Mom told me I got my dad's social security because he died in action. It couldn't have been since he never existed. Who had paid for the place in Florida, the home in St. Charles, and all the other things we had? No way could it have been bought on a teacher's salary. People always said could tell a child anything and they would believe it. I learned a lesson: well-cared for child doesn't question anything.

I had so many questions.

Ryan must have stopped. I had walked another quarter of a mile before I noticed I was alone. I turned and walked back to him.

"Would you like to share any of those thoughts and memories with me?"

"I was going over some things about my childhood that don't add up. I feel foolish for not questioning anything before now."

He pulled me to him and buried his chin in my hair. "You always smell so good." His chest was warm against me. He took a long deep breath and a sigh escaped before he continued. "Adults have manipulated children for years and some always will. Kids believe anything that is repeated time and time again. In your case there were secrets. I'd like to see this go well for you and your mom without too many strong words or accusations. What gums up the story the most is her not knowing about the other child. It's pretty far-fetched."

I didn't answer. I agreed with him. She had to know there were two of us. Who separates twins at birth? Why?

Ryan's parents were killed in a car crash when he was sixteen. It had to have been devastating to him. I asked myself if I had a right to be upset about the things I learned. The answer banged around in my head—absolutely.

I turned toward the ocean, took Ryan's hand and tried to convey my thoughts. Several minutes passed. "Let's go back to the condo."

We walked back in a peaceful silence.

CHAPTER 15

Mom sat at the table on the deck. She looked rested and not as stressed as the night before. There were bagels, cream cheese and coffee in a carafe on a table behind her. I smiled at her.

She reached behind her to touch my arm while I served myself. "Should we wait for Ryan?"

"That would be great, Mom. I won't have to tell him everything."

"Did I hear my name?" We both looked toward him.

There wasn't any small talk. Mom was ready to tell her story and we were ready to listen.

"Okay, as I told you last night. I was a surgical nurse at a private hospital. I knew some high profile people moved through there. They paid the staff twice as much as the other hospitals. They never urged me to do anything out of the ordinary. One day, well evening, I was at home and Dr. Signorelli called. He was the head of surgery. He called me in to help him deal with an accident."

She stopped to refill her coffee cup. "It was the beginning of maybe fifteen times over the years I assisted in procedures on patients who were never admitted. They received the treatment they needed and moved on with no records. I'm sure the names they used were not real. In my pay envelope, along with my regular salary, were large amounts of cash. He made me feel needed. I rented a safe deposit box and put the cash in it. I knew I couldn't go out and spend it. Everyone watched that hospital. By everyone, I mean the FBI. Every day there was a surveillance van parked outside taking pictures of who came and went."

Mom stood and walked around the porch as she talked. "Everyone knew I wanted a child. You can't work closely with the same people day after day and they not know your true heart.

"One night the phone rang and they asked me to come in. There were only two other people in Dr. Signorelli's office, a nurse from the pediatric unit and you. The nurse handed you to me and left. You were the most beautiful thing I'd ever seen, with a fuzz of bright red hair and a gurgle when you looked at me. They gave me a birth certificate and a sizeable amount of money. The certificate of birth listed your father as John Madison."

Mom stopped talking and turned to stare at me.

I narrowed my eyes. "You changed your story. Last night John Madison was the boyfriend of a friend of yours and you took the picture. Which is it?"

"This is the truth. You had me flustered last night. If you're going to badger me, I'll stop right here."

We stared at one another. I didn't move a muscle.

She looked at her hands. "There isn't much more. We moved to St. Charles and I told everyone I was a widow. No one questioned it. When you were in the third grade, I bought this place and we came here whenever we could. Right or wrong, Kate, I didn't hesitate. I had the baby I wanted and a plausible story about where you came from. When I questioned who John Madison was, I was told *whoever you want him to be*."

I shook my head at her. "I wonder what happened to Sophie. Who took her? This sounds like science fiction."

"We know more than we did." Ryan stood. "You were both born in St. Louis at Honor Hospital on April 1, 1980. That information should get us something. I figure there was another woman who wanted a child too. She got Sophie. If your mother didn't see the birth mother she could have been kept in the dark about the second child."

"I only wish Sophie had come to me sooner. She must have known about me for a long time. I wish she wasn't in trouble with the law. She told me she could explain it away, but never came to me. As my grandmother was supposed to have said, *if wishes were horses beggars would ride."*

Ryan stood between Mom and me.

Mom wept. "Can you ever forgive me, Kate?"

I went to her. "At this point I must forgive you, not to would be harder on me than you. I need some time to absorb it all; to find out everything in my life is different than I thought is disturbing. You're sure my mother's name was Julia Lombardi?"

She took my hand. "No Kate, your mother's name is and always has been Denise Madison. The woman who carried you died before you were born."

The truth of her statement hung in the room like stagnant fog.

Ryan broke the spell. "Denise, what was your real name?"

Mom glanced from me to Ryan. Her face had drained of all color. It was obviously a question she didn't expect. She chose to dance around it. "I don't know if there is anyone alive any more who even cares about what happened thirty-five years ago, but if there is, I don't want to end up in the ocean as fish food."

"If I find out your given name, it puts you in danger? Who would I tell?"

She sat quietly. So much time had passed; I didn't think she would tell us. "Louise Dawson. You have no idea what you are doing by bringing this out in the open. "

"If you tell me why it was and is so important to hide all of this, then maybe I can understand," I said.

"Someone had to know there was a second baby," Ryan insisted. Maybe they thought she was still born. Maybe the baby was promised to someone else and when they found out there were two children, they panicked and gave the other one to you. May I see Kate's birth certificate?"

"Yes, of course, I have a copy, but Kate has the original. I told you it has me listed as her mother and John as her father."

"Indulge me," Ryan grinned.

Mom got up. "Sure, I'll get it."

I sat at the table and studied the waves. I found the ocean to be a metaphor of life and the world. It changed every second. As the waves lapped the shore and went out again, they left behind a piece of the old and took some of the new. It was either going in or out or up or down. It sustained itself. I needed to be more like the ocean, to remember the beauty of my past, that with my loss of Michael, I found Ryan. When I found Lizzy Smith, I left behind my stubborn selfishness and made room for my adorable Chili.

I had a sister. I saw her up close. She shared a pathway to my soul and she needed help. It was essential I find her.

Ryan took a picture of my birth certificate with his phone. "It says here your maiden name was Denise Jones, not very imaginative."

I turned my attention from the ocean to him and my mother. One thing was for sure, the older I got the less I understood life and its twists and turns. "So which is it, Jones or Dawson?"

She looked down and didn't answer. She had more secrets hidden and she wouldn't share.

We caught an evening plane back to St. Louis. I didn't have anything to say. Ryan didn't talk either. I took the time and went over the entire visit one scene at a time. I wanted to see if I remembered anything I didn't pick up on earlier.

I bet my birth mother didn't know about me either. I took out my notepad and made my own notes. I wrote down the need to find out who else worked at Honor Hospital. Who ended up with a baby? If he was still alive I needed to find the doctor who signed my birth certificate and a nurse named Sally Jeffers, who signed as a witness. I wanted to know why I had never heard of Honor Hospital. By the time the plane landed, I had over thirty 'find outs' on my list.

Ryan drove me back to the apartment but instead of coming in he told me he had an appointment and would be home later. Secretly, I was pleased. I wanted more alone time to review and reminisce about a childhood that wasn't as it had seemed.

I could only think so much before I had gone around the circle several times. My mom never married. She took a baby from a dead mafia princess. A baby who would most likely have ended up in the child welfare system and might have had twenty foster homes and none of the advantages I had. She took money to stay quiet about the child's identity, and likely, the people who were involved in it were either dead or had moved on to something different. For thirty-four years, Mom and I lived a life above suspicion about anything or anyone.

It played repeatedly in my mind. I silently hashed out the different ways my life could have been. With everything I learned at Mom's I decided I loved what she did for me. Everything she did was illegal. I could only hope she had done what she did for the right reasons. Somewhere I had a real mother and father.

The same fact came up over and over. My mother was paid a large sum of money to take me. Someone sold me. It made me shudder.

Sophie called again. "It's me" She had my voice, but more hoarse and with an Eastern US dialect.

"Where are you?"

"I can't tell you. It would put you in great danger. Have you been with your mother all this time? Did she tell you we are the biggest secret ever?"

"Sophie, I don't believe anyone would care after all these years. Mom's sixty-four and teaches grade school math in Florida. How could it hurt anyone if we found each other now?"

"Kate, you're naïve, and apparently you have no idea who our so-called father is or where I've been all my life. Come to 2456 S. Chamberlain, Apartment 34, be there at seven-thirty tomorrow evening. Come alone and don't let yourself be followed. I'll tell you all I know. If we pool our knowledge we might have the answers.

She hung up.

I was both excited and scared. Something told me I was in no danger if I went. I planned to be there.

Alone.

CHAPTER 16

Ryan called about nine and wanted to know if I was hungry for Mexican food. I told him I had been dreaming of a comfort meal I had when I was a kid. "Be there in thirty minutes,"

I went to the kitchen and began putting the meal together. I heard the elevator come to the top floor exactly thirty minutes later.

I stood outside the door as it opened. "Hi."

He reached for me, hugged me rakishly and held me back at arm's length. "Is our comfort food ready? I'm hungry."

I took his free hand. "Yes, it's ready."

When he looked down he smiled. "Tuna sandwiches and tomato soup? It's one of my favorites too. Another one I like is chili and a peanut butter sandwich."

We laughed. "Wine sounded horrible with this, so I poured milk."

"It's perfect, Kate, and so are you."

We wolfed down the food. Butterflies flew around in my stomach. It wasn't the food. It was that I was to meet Sophie and I hadn't told him. I had never lied to him before. Well, not a lie exactly; an omission. Omissions led to lies and lies led to lack of trust, which led to the end of a relationship. I decided I had to tell him.

I waited until we moved to the couch and we each had a glass of wine. "Sophie called earlier." He waited for the rest. "She gave me an address and wants me to meet her tomorrow evening."

"That's great. Some of my men will surround the place and we'll have her where we want her."

I laid my hand lightly on his arm. "We can't do that. I promised I would come alone without being followed."

"Kate!" He put his glass on the coffee table and stood. "You don't really think I'm going to let you go meet a strange woman, a murder suspect, alone, do you?"

I looked up at him. "It's what I think and it's what I expect."

"This is a hard one. How can I let you go into danger without going along?"

"Ryan, sit down." He did, but only on the edge of the seat. "I have good instincts. I don't feel like there's any danger here. She's my twin. I sense the connection. She wouldn't hurt me. I don't know why the man was killed, but I believe her when she says she didn't do it. She wants to talk and I need answers."

We sat in silence. I heard the elevator go down and the speaker come to life. Amy came to drop Chili off. I ran to the lift. A face-lick from my dog could fix the worst of situations.

The door opened and there they stood. Chili wiggled from head to toe. Digger ran to Ryan and jumped in his lap. I felt the tension exhale from the room. "Come in."

Chili jumped and turned every time I reached for her. She jumped back and ran in a circle. She was one happy dog. "Are you hungry?"

"Oh, no, Jake's in the car. We're having a late dinner tonight. He leaves for Dallas in the morning. Are you coming to work?"

"Sure, I'll be there around nine. Anything happen while Ryan and I were in Florida?"

"No, not really. Nathan and I make a good team. There's money in the bank and we've found one runaway girl and three lost dogs, the usual boring stuff."

"Okay, got to go. Come on Digger Dog!" The dog was reluctant to jump down as Ryan rubbed his belly. When the door opened, it reinforced Amy was leaving, he ran to the elevator like a bullet. I saw Ryan wave goodbye.

I scooped Chili up in my arms and walked back to the couch. Ryan held out his hands to take her. "Tell you what I'll do," I offered. "I'll give you the address. You'll do nothing with it. If you don't hear from me by midnight you can go there and do what you feel you need to do. Until midnight I need to have my freedom."

"Ten."

"Eleven." I countered

He rubbed Chili's ears "Ten o'clock or no deal."

"Fine, Ryan, but if you do anything before ten, I'll never speak to you again."

"Deal." We sealed it with a kiss, or two, and more.

The next day we found out there were five babies born at Honor Hospital from March twenty-ninth through April second, 1980? Four of them were girls. They were Diane, June, Shirley, and Daisy. No baby named Kate, Kathryn or Kathleen or anything remotely close.

To make things more confusing, there had never been a nurse named Sally Jeffers, and no Dr. Signorelli worked there within the fifteen years before or after I was born.

"I'll ask Sophia who's listed on her birth certificate as delivery nurse, doctor, and parents." My mother was never registered as a nurse in any state at any time. She had graduated from Lindenwood University in St. Charles, Missouri in 1975 with a double major in Education and Spanish. It matched the profession she had now, but why she lied about being a surgical nurse was another inconsistency to add to the pile.

Further investigation brought up a Denise Madison from St. Charles who died in a car crash the night of her high school graduation in 1970.

There was no activity on her Social Security number, and she had no credit cards, driver's license, or bank records until she graduated from college in 1975. In my occupation, I'd seen it a dozen times. Someone needed an identity so they visited a cemetery or searched court records until they found a person who died young. They claimed their identity and began a new life, another lie by my *mother.*

We still didn't know anything about Sophie. I hoped to answer all of my questions when I saw her.

There was a death certificate issued May 17, 1982, for a Julia Lombardi. She died in New Jersey, not in St. Louis, and not in an automobile accident. She died in an airplane crash along with most of her high school volleyball team, she was fifteen.

The one fact I had that couldn't be disputed—everything my mother told us in Florida was a lie.

I had hoped to find out more about my sister before we met, but clearly, it wasn't meant to happen. We headed home. Ryan sat on the chair in the bedroom and chatted with me as I attempted to get dressed.

"Are you going to wear that?" He looked at my black dress and matching jacket. "Are you planning on ending up out on the town?"

Instead of lashing out, I smiled.

"I think slacks and a jacket so you can carry your gun."

He did have a point. I settled on a pair of man-tailored navy pants with a muted plaid jacket. My shoulder holster was well covered. Ryan seemed pleased.

He gave me all sorts of advice and pointers on how to protect myself. I felt like a young girl on her first date. He seemed to have forgotten I was a trained detective.

At six-thirty, I headed for the south side of St. Louis. The homes there were beautiful yet only a rifle shot from one of the worst areas in the city. Such was the face of St. Louis.

It didn't seem to bother anyone. There were outside café's and farmer's markets, specialty shops, and the waterfront within five miles. I had entered the address into my GPS before I pulled out of the parking lot at the apartment.

Thirty-four wasn't an apartment at all, but a three-story brownstone, no wider than a back alley. There was an entire row of them, all numbered oddly. Sophie's number was neatly tucked between number seventeen and twenty-two.

I wanted to learn the real story of my life.

The parking lot sat nine or ten houses past where I wanted to be. It was dark and on the other side of the street. Signs everywhere let you know that parking in front of the row of dwellings was strictly prohibited.

When I drove into the lot I realized it was private and meant only for inhabitants and guests. I pulled into a spot marked with the number she gave me. On one side sat a new Jaguar. The other space that shared the number sat empty.

It was a spooky walk to the door. There were three steps up to a small stoop. When I touched the door to knock, it creaked open. I pulled my gun and looked through the apartment one room at a time.

The living room was in a shambles, the bedroom door had been kicked in. I could hear running water in the bathroom so I pushed the door. It wasn't latched and slammed open into the body of a man. I looked around and holstered my weapon. A touch informed me the man was dead. He hadn't been there long. He was warm.

I took a deep breath and tried to decide who to call first, Roger or Ryan. I decided on Roger. After the strange things that had happened to me recently, I wanted to cover my butt. The smell of warm, fresh blood made me gag. I wanted to find out who he was but decided to wait on the porch and not contaminate the scene.

Two men sprang from nowhere and grabbed me. I tried to scream, but one put his hand over my mouth. The other one took my Glock and cell phone out of my jacket pocket and tossed them on the front porch along with my keys, ID, and the money I carried in my back pocket.

They shoved me into the backseat of a car with a man who was so big he took up most of the space. "Settle down, Sophia. You knew we'd find you and take you back. The old man will be angry if you have any bruises.

"Let me go, I'm not Sophia. I'm Kate Nash. Please, you're making a big mistake."

"We could always leave you here and make it look like you killed someone else. As it is now, you'll look like another victim."

"Here, take this, it'll make the trip more bearable." The big man next to me poured a sour liquid into my mouth. I almost choked as I tried not to swallow it. It was the last thing I remembered until I woke up sometime later in the dark.

CHAPTER 17

My head pounded as if someone had hit me in the head with a sledgehammer. The dark was so black, it occurred to me I might be buried in a hole. I didn't want to panic and use all of my air in case I'd been entombed.

When I tried to stretch, there was plenty of room. I slid around and realized I was on a bed and not restrained. I couldn't see an inch in front of me. I stood and took tiny steps until something solid hit my hands, which I'd managed to extend in front of me. I turned and touched my way to what I decided was a window. I opened the heavy drapes. It looked as though I was on the second floor. The window I gazed out appeared to face the back of some kind of compound.

Satisfied I had seen all I could from where I stood, I turned my attention to the inside of the room. The light drifted in from the yard lights and bathed the room in a warm glow. The decorations were pretty but outdated. The drapes were a muted mauve. White carpet with roses covered the floor except for a small area in front of what appeared to be a wood burning fireplace.

The sitting area sported a couch, love seat, chair, and ottoman all in a deep rose color. Everything looked like décor right out of a 1940's Alfred Hitchcock movie.

On the wall behind the area, two more windows stretched floor to ceiling. I walked over, knelt on the love seat and pulled the cord.

There were more lights in what I gauged it to be the front. The gate was so far away from the house, I had to concentrate to make it out. Once my eyes adjusted to the dim lights surrounding the place, I saw four men with guns behind a tall wrought iron gate. Though I could only see a limited distance, I got the feeling the stone wall I saw encircled the perimeter of the estate.

I went back to the first window. There was an area the size of two football fields filled with cars. Cadillacs, Fords, Nissans, were neatly backed against the wall.

There was no doubt in my mind that I had been kidnapped and taken to the family home in Newark. I didn't know what to expect and the unknown terrified me. I'd have to mingle and interact with organized crime if I wanted to gain my freedom. If I wanted to survive this I couldn't let it intimidate me.

My concentration was interrupted by a soft knock on the door. It hadn't dawned on me to see if the door was locked. Before I could take a step toward the door, it opened and a middle-aged woman floated in. She was short, shorter than me. Her skirt touched the floor giving the illusion she had no feet. She held a covered tray in her arms. It looked heavy. I moved closer, took it away from her and sat it on a table to my left.

She turned on the lights. "Sophia. I'm glad you're back. Your father has threatened all of us if we didn't find you. How could you put us all in such danger? You know how important this wedding is to the future of the *families*." She had stuck both hands under her apron. She looked like a small, Italian, Aunt Jemima.

A thousand questions swirled around in my brain, but I decided to let her think I was Sophia.

"I know it's important to my father." It was a terrible chance to take, to try to be someone I wasn't. Someone I knew nothing about. My instincts told me it was a better choice than to tell her who I was and cause more trouble for myself.

She looked at me so intently, my body got hot with fear. "Who are you?"

"Don't you recognize me? It's me, Sophie."

She shook her head and pulled a cell phone out of her pocket. She dialed a number "Anthony. I need you in Sophia's room right away."

My knees buckled. How had I given myself away so easily? I pulled out a chair and sat. "Are you going to turn me in?"

"Not at this point, but don't insult my intelligence. All one has to do is hear you talk to know you don't belong here. When Tony gets up here, I suggest you tell the truth." She spoke with a thick Italian accent.

I gulped. "Who's Anthony?"

She pointed her finger at me. "He is my son and Sophia's protector and best friend. It would be in your best interest not to lie to him. He knows her better than anyone."

The door opened without the courtesy of a knock. A tall, Navy Seal sort of man dressed in expensive clothes stepped in. He closed the door and locked it behind him. He walked over to me and looked me up and down. His mouth curved into a cynical smile. "You must be Sophie's twin, Kate. It is you isn't it Kate?"

I lowered my head and let it rest in my hands. "Yes, but I didn't come to scam anyone. How do you know about me? I thought Sophie having a sister was the biggest secret in the country." I had a tendency to ramble when I was scared, but I didn't care. "Three men, dressed like you picked me up as I was on my way to meet Sophie at an address she gave me. They drugged me and I woke up here. I don't even know what day it is."

He looked at his mother who shook her head in agreement. "She's telling the truth. I got a call from the office that told me she was home. Of course, they wouldn't know she's a fake."

Tony turned away from his mother and looked my way. "What day were you supposed to meet her?"

Before I could answer, someone else was at the door. Tony answered the door, talked quietly with whoever it was for a moment before turning his attention back to me. "To keep both you and Sophie safe, you'll have to be Sophie until we can find her. I believe, if she was supposed to meet you and you didn't show up, she'll put together what happened, and she'll come home immediately. In the meantime you'll have to be her."

I stood and walked closer to him. "There is more to it. I found a dead man in the bathroom at the house where we were to meet and Sophia was nowhere around."

I watched the color of the man's face changed from tan and healthy to white and concerned. "Again, I need to ask when that was."

"Tuesday evening the seventeenth."

He looked toward his mother. "Two days ago I don't like this."

I fell back into my chair. "I don't either; can't I just wait in the room until she shows up?" I obviously hadn't fooled Tony or his mother. How in the world could I fool anyone else?

Tony came and sat next to me. "It isn't that simple. Right now, your soon to be husband is in the study with your father and they're waiting for you." He looked at his mother. "Mom, lay out something for Kate to wear."

He turned his attention back to me. "The biggest difference between you two is the way you speak. She was raised in New Jersey and has a distinct dialect. Your best bet is to say little or nothing. If you must talk, try to mimic her. I'll give you a quick background. Your fiancé is Johnny Lombardi. Your father, Dominic De Marco, thinks a marriage between the two of you will create a lasting peace between the two organized crime families, one of which Sophie was born into. You better change and go down. The study is the first door on the right at the bottom of the stairs. I'll be back later to talk about what we're going to do."

He paused at the door and walked back to me. "The other noticeable difference is how you move. Your moves are casual. You're loose. Sophia carries herself with a regal air" He stepped closer to me and put a hand on each of my shoulders. He gently pressed my arms close together. She's more closed up. She always sits with her hands on her lap. Like this." Tony sat without crossing his legs. He moved them closer together and tucked them under the chair. He rested both hands on his knees, one on top of the other. "She also walks and sits ramrod straight. The only other glaring difference is; Sophie is left-handed. It'll be difficult for you, but try to remember to reach and eat with your left hand. I doubt there will be any food to worry about tonight. This is all a lot to remember. Good luck. We can only pray Sophie gets here soon. You'd better hurry."

The clothes Rosa laid out were fine. With them she included a pair of flat-heeled Mary Janes. I dressed quickly and went downstairs. Someone was engaged in a conversation and it wasn't cordial. I followed the sound. When I stepped into the room, I saw two men. I had to lock my knees to keep them from banging together.

One man wore an expensive silk smoking jacket, the other in a black suit. He looked like he was dressed to attend a funeral. I took a chance and walked toward the man in the lounging coat and kissed his cheek. "Father." I almost choked on the word as it left my mouth.

"Glad you graced us with your presence, Sophia." He didn't hide his contempt for my tardiness. "Johnny has been chomping at the bit to see you."

For the first time, I gave my attention to the man who sat on the other side of the room, where he sucked on a fat, smelly cigar. He smiled at me. He had to be in his late sixties and it was now clear to me why Rosa had laid out low heeled shoes. When he stood to take my hand, he came to my shoulder. A man who was shorter than me, it was a first.

He took a seat on the couch and patted the space beside him. "Come, sit by me, dear."

My mind spun, but my lips smiled. The next hour was torture. I had heard about *the short man syndrome* or the *Napoleon complex* as Ryan called it. Now I saw it firsthand. He was a bully and a braggart. I didn't have to worry about what to say or how to say it, he monopolized the entire conversation. Dominic said no more than a polite yes or no now and then.

No wonder Sophia had run away.

Johnny wanted to go to Italy on our honeymoon. I decided to agree to anything. I was sure I could never have married him. If Sophie was anything like me, I couldn't see her married to him either.

I left my father in the study. I had never uttered the word *father* in relation to myself. I walked Johnny to the front door. He stood on his tip toes and kissed my cheek before he left. I wanted to wipe it off.

When I got back to the study, my *father* looked at me. I got nervous. I prayed he didn't want to talk about something I knew nothing about. Was there something about me he recognized that made him know I wasn't Sophia?

He'd moved while I was gone, and was seated behind his desk with his hands one on top of the other. "Have a seat, Sophia, we haven't spoken in awhile."

I perched on the edge of the chair closest to him and folded my hands in my lap. I sat up as straight as I could. I remained silent. He never moved his gaze from my face. It was obvious we were in a negotiation. I didn't know much about them, but the one who spoke first, lost, so I sat.

After what seemed like an eternity, he smiled at me. "Very good, Sophia. Some of what I taught you seems to have stuck. My dear girl, I don't think you trust me. I told you the marriage between the two families is a necessity. I will see that it doesn't last one more day than it has to. You need to behave like an adult and stay here until you fulfill your commitment."

This was where I knew I could get into real trouble.

"Because you are my only child, I'm going to try to approach this in a different way. There aren't many *families* left, and none as profitable as ours. When you were growing up, it was known that we, the De Marco's, were the ones in charge. It's not that way anymore. It hasn't been since Johnny's father passed away. Stephan and I could work together—we never had a war between us. Johnny's a hot head. In order to keep our businesses together, we have to join the two families into one. Do you not get that?"

"Yes." I didn't trust my accent to say more. I wanted to. He slammed his hand on the desktop.

I either said it in a defiant tone or looked at him some way I shouldn't have. He slammed his hand on the desk with such force it moved his paperweight. "I'm only going to tell you this one more time. If you do not cooperate, I will keep you under lock and key until the wedding."

Tears rolled down my cheeks. I didn't care if it wasn't me, it was horrible.

"Sophia, Johnny will have us all murdered in our sleep if he thinks this wedding won't happen. As soon as the rest of the Lombardi family realizes who and what he is, I will earn their trust and loyalty and he will no longer present a problem for us. He is an evil man."

I crossed my arms over my chest and stayed determined not to lash out. "I understand."

He stood. "For the next month, until the wedding, you'll not leave your room without a bodyguard. If you run away one more time, I'll make good on my threat to lock you up. I have already lost one good man because you were in St. Louis instead of here." With that, he was gone.

I sat back in the chair and took a deep breath. I took another breath and used the side arms of the chair to help me up. I was afraid.

I prayed that the other night when I didn't make it home, Ryan went to look for me. He had the address, and my car most likely sat in the same place I left it. I remembered the dead body. Sophia might have needed to be rescued too.

CHAPTER 18

Tony was in my room when I got back. "It must have gone all right, you're still alive."

I walked past him and sat at the table. "I don't find any of this funny. Is it possible to get something to eat? It's been at least two days. My stomach is about to rebel. I don't think I can keep up this charade. I am sure people are searching for me. What if Sophie doesn't make it back here?"

He sat next to me. "One thing at a time, yes, I'll have a tray sent up. There's no doubt in my mind that Sophie will know exactly what to do. She'll be here when she can get here."

He took his phone out and called for someone to bring a dinner tray to Miss Sophie's room. While we waited, he talked to me about how to stay out of trouble. "You have no choice here. I'm not sure what Dominic would do if he realized you aren't Sophia. It would be easier for us all if we knew why they separated you in the first place." In a softer voice he added. "I can't let myself believe he would do any harm to you if he did find out."

"You're the only one of us that thinks that. He has mean eyes. Do you think Sophie will call?"

Hard to say, the entire estate's covered with recording and surveillance equipment. It's difficult to have a conversation with no one listening in."

He sat with me while I ate. The way he stared at me, I guessed he tried to find more differences between my sister and me. I was curious myself. "So aren't you worried about someone listening in and finding out I'm not Sophie? Do you see the differences?"

He smiled at me. "Your first question, I swept the room for bugs earlier. The answer to your second question, there are subtle differences. Only someone as close to her as I am could tell the difference."

I didn't want to be nosey, but I had to ask. "Just how close are you?"

He leaned his chair back so it balanced on the two back legs. He fidgeted like a twelve-year-old. "As close as two people can be. Until Dominic came up with the idea to save *The Family* by forcing a marriage between her and Johnny, we were to marry next year."

"And Dominic was going to allow that to happen?"

He laughed but it sounded anything but happy. "The only job Sophia does here are some petty court cases when one of the soldiers gets too rough with someone or Dominic wants to buy or sell real estate. He has kept her out of the criminal enterprises. We were going to ask him if we could go. She thought he would let us. I believed he would never let it happen."

"So she's an attorney?"

"Yes, we both went to Rutgers."

"Talk to me about her."

"I went to school when she was three. She waited patiently by the door every day for me to come home and play with her. She always wanted to play school. I wasn't crazy about it, but all she had to do was smile at me and she got her way."

"Even when she was a child?" I asked.

He let his chair down with a thud. "Oh yes, even then. She went to parochial girl's school, Oak Knoll School of the Holy Child for elementary and St. Vincent's Academy for high school. She was chauffeured there, walked inside and they picked up at the door at the end of the day.

"I'd better go. We'll talk more tomorrow. Try to relax. I'll coach you through this until she shows up. I tried to call her earlier. Her phone goes straight to voicemail. It makes my stomach hurt to wonder why she doesn't answer."

Tony didn't linger. I sat for a while and thought about my sister, where she could be, and how different our childhoods had been.

I knew it wasn't right, but I searched the room. I peeked in her desk drawers. Her day planner was open wide. She hadn't recorded much, just outings with Tony, dinners with Johnny and Dominic, and times she needed to be in court.

Rose came in with a tray. She put it on the table and walked out.

In the center drawer in her desk I found a box of business cards-

Sophia De Marco. Esquire.
Representing De Marco Enterprises, Inc.

Her high school and college transcripts were in a package in the bottom drawer as well as some personal cards for her early birthdays and holidays. They were signed, *with all my love, Roxy.* The return addresses were all the same, Roxy Watkins, c/o Ritz-Carlton, New York, Battery Park.

I looked around the room for some sort of electronic device I could use to research what I now knew. It was hopeless; I had no phone, no iPad or laptop. Maybe it was for the best. If the place was as secure as Tony made it out to be, I could get myself in a mess of trouble for digging into things that were none of my business.

It was difficult to sleep. I missed Ryan, my precious Chili, Amy, my bed, and everything familiar to me. It had been three days, where were they? I couldn't believe it could be difficult for Sophie to come home. I would think she could walk directly through the front gate. The longer this went on, the more chance there would be that my true identity could be discovered. I tossed and turned, sleep never came.

Dominic made it clear he didn't expect Sophie to remain married to Johnny. Chills ran down my back as I thought of the different scenarios that could play out. My imagination ran away with me. Dominic was domineering and cold. I couldn't believe he was my father.

Rosa brought my breakfast in the next morning. I asked her where Tony was. "He will come up when he can." The phone in my room rang. I watched it for a few seconds as though it would entertain me with a trick. I picked it up.

"Your father wants you to join him in the dining room at eight this evening for dinner." The man on the other end of the conversation didn't give me time to answer. I guessed *no* was not an option. The clock on the wall indicated it was only one. I prayed Tony made it back to talk to me before I had to go downstairs.

The confidence I had when I first got there had been replaced with fear and questions. Where was Sophie, and Ryan, and Amy? My churning stomach convinced me something was wrong, very wrong. I was in a role completely out of my range. I was an investigator. Part of my job had always been to be strong and in control to help someone who was out of control and scared. Now I was the one who got hung up in a situation where all I could do was to get pulled along.

There was a light tap on my door at five-forty. I rushed to open it hoping Tony stood on the other side. He did. I stuck my head out and looked both ways, before pulling him inside. "I have to be in the dining room in at eight to join Dominic for dinner. I don't know what to wear, what to do, or what to say."

He stepped into the room and closed the door behind him. "Calm down. It'll be fine. There's a simple blue dress in the closet. Put it on, pull your hair back, or maybe in a bun if you can manage it. I would get Mom to help you, but there isn't time and I am all thumbs. When you enter the dining room, walk to the chair nearest him on his right. Don't sit until he sits and Randle pulls the chair out for you. I don't think he'll talk to you. He often would have dinner with Sophie and never say a word. Other times he was talkative and almost normal.

"If he says anything, think before you answer. Make sure you use your New Jersey voice. Her resonance is much lower than yours. Try to remember that. If he orders a drink after dinner, there is something he wants to tell you or ask you. Best agree with him. It'll shorten the evening. If he doesn't order a drink, he'll abruptly leave without a word to you. Don't get up until he is gone and Randle comes over to help you up. Do you have it?"

"I think so." I rubbed my head, trying to soak it all in.

"Remember, you're a southpaw."

He put one of his hands on each of my shoulders and smiled. "I know you do. Now get dressed and go. You have ten minutes to meet Randle at the bottom of the stairs. I'll see you when you get back."

Breathe I told myself. Before I opened the door, I took two more calming breaths.

When I reached the top of the staircase, Randle stood at the bottom. His face remained expressionless.

The first part went as Tony described. Once I was seated, a maid brought soup. Dominic and I ate in silence. The quiet gave me an opportunity to focus on how I ate and sat. I strived not to make any more noise than necessary. I gutted my way through the soup, salad, meatloaf, baked potato and green beans. My shoulders relaxed a little with the realization it would soon be over. Desert was my all time favorite, Cherries Jubilee. But tonight it was just one more thing to draw out the torture. I wasn't used to using my left hand. The only good thing was it slowed down my eating and made me pay more attention.

When a servant came in to clear the dessert dishes from the table, I breathed a sigh of relief. Dominic didn't summon anyone to pour him a drink.

I heard a noise and looked toward the door. When I looked back he was gone.

Randle appeared and touched the back of my chair. He escorted me to the bottom of the staircase where he had met me earlier. For the first time, he spoke. "Have a pleasant night, Miss Sophia."

"Thank you, Randle, I will."

CHAPTER 19

Tony came by after breakfast and suggested we get out of the house for awhile.

I didn't hesitate to nod my head. "I don't have any money or ID. When the men took me in St. Louis, they took everything I had."

"Let me find out if anyone knows about your belongings. I'll be back soon."

I showered and put on some casual clothes I found in the closet. My sister had more dressy clothes than I. It was more difficult to dress down. I found something and waited for Tony to come back. "The men didn't bring any of it with them. They left it in your car. I'm sorry."

"I can replace it. But my Glock would make me feel safer. Where're we going?"

"Do you always carry a gun?"

"Yes, I'm a Private Investigator."

He sat at the table and faced me. "You can catch the bad guys and Sophie can prosecute them."

I put my hand on his arm as a friendly gesture. "We wouldn't have to go far to find them, would we?"

Tony didn't acknowledge my last comment. He changed the subject. "My plan is to go to the mall. There's a real coffee shop. You could get a latte. A change of scenery and a chance to be yourself would relax you. We can go to a movie if you like."

My coat was on the bed. He helped me put it on. "The mall sounds wonderful. It doesn't solve my money problems though."

"I'll take care of everything. I forget you aren't familiar with the De Marco money. Dominic pays Sophie a six-figure salary to get petty criminals out of speeding tickets, misdemeanors, and assaults. Apparently, she doesn't need to be here to earn it."

We went out the back door where a man greeted us by name and with a friendly smile. "Do you and Miss Sophia need a car?"

"Yes, Mike. We'll be out a few hours."

The young man jogged out of sight and returned with a shiny black Cadillac. He slipped out of the driver's seat and rushed around to my side to help me in. Since he appeared so friendly, I thanked him by name.

I relaxed as we approached the gate. Tony stopped when an armed man walked up to his window. He lowered it and spoke to him. "Hi Sam, Miss Sophia and I are on our way to the mall and maybe a movie."

"Does Mr. De Marco know about this? We have strict orders not to let her off the grounds without a bodyguard."

Tony leaned out the window. "Yes, I spoke to him last night. My butt is on the line if I don't have her back by dark."

The guard took a step backward. "Sorry, just doing my job."

He opened the gate and we drove through. The driveway was about a mile long. At the end of it, on the left, was a concrete circle with a high stone wall around it. There was an Essex County Sheriff's car with two officers in it. Farther around the same drive was a dirty tan van with a huge anten-na and blacked out windows.

Before I had a chance to ask, Tony explained. "The Sheriff has a car stationed here twenty-four-seven. They keep track of who leaves, what car they're driving, and they run the plates. Our informants say they keep a log of our comings and goings."

I had been in law enforcement long enough to know this sort of thing was standard procedure with gangs. During the stakeouts I took part in, we were never so blatant. I also had never been involved in a Mafia investigation. "Who's in the van?"

"The FBI, they take pictures of who comes and goes. No privacy around here. Sometimes one of our moles takes his turn and brings back most of their findings."

"And Sophie has lived with this her entire life? Hard to imagine."

I was on edge the rest of the day. I wondered who might have been behind us or took our picture as we strolled around the mall. I hoped some of Ryan's men would show up.

We didn't talk much. It did me good to get away from the De Marco stronghold for a few hours.

Our first stop was the coffee shop. I sat at a table in the back while Tony ordered and brought our drinks back. My heart jumped in my chest when looked toward the door and there stood Amy peeking in the window. My neck and shoulders relaxed. I had a sensation of relief when I saw my friend.

She came in, ordered, and sat at the table adjacent to us. I leaned across the table. The dark-haired woman seated to my left is Amy, my business partner. I need to talk to her without anyone eavesdropping. What should we do?"

"I'll take care of it. I'll act like she dropped something and I'll return it to her."

He reached down to the floor and came up with a ten dollar bill in his hand as though he had found it. He stood, walked to Amy and offered it to her. I couldn't hear their exchange but she smiled, took the money, said *thank you*, put the money in her purse, and went back to drinking her coffee. Tony came back to our table. "She'll meet you in the dressing room at Sassy Design. Sophie likes that store so it won't look out of the ordinary if someone's watching. Finish your drink and don't hurry. Tell me about your business. Lean toward me when you talk. Put your hand on mine and laugh once in a while. It'll make it look like we're still in love."

The next ten minutes were torturous. All I wanted to do was to go to the shop and talk to Amy.

Tony and I glanced around the shop. He picked up a couple of dresses and showed them to me. I did the same. We agreed on an emerald green sheath we both liked and I took it to the dressing room. He sat on a bench directly to the right of the door so he could see who came and went.

I didn't know whether to try on the dress or not. It seemed like I had been in the room forever and no Amy. I was about to give up when she slipped through the door. She stood on the chair so it looked like there was only one person in the room. "I was beginning to think you would never come to rescue me."

"That isn't why I'm here. We're going to have to leave you there a few more days. When they took you from your sister's apartment she was hiding near the side of the building. Earlier, she had gone there to wait for you and walked into a murder scene. She was frightened she would be charged with the killing so she hid. She was hidden in the shadows near the side of the building. She wanted to save you but Ryan showed up. Once they all realized what happened, they made plans to try to come get you. The dead man was a member of a *family* called Lombardi. Are you familiar?" She didn't wait for me to answer. "Sophie thinks someone from that *family* killed the man to make it look like she did it. Someone grabbed her and roughed her up pretty good. She can't go home until the noticeable injuries are healed enough to be hidden by make-up. I came to give you an untraceable track phone, and a gun."

"It's a wonder I'm not dead. Tony and his mother knew right away I wasn't Sophie. If Dominic finds out, I shudder to think what might happen."

She reached down and hugged me. "I'm sorry. Ryan has done his best. He's in the van at the end of the drive. One of his contacts got him in. Sophie's afraid for you, but she knew Tony would protect you. I think in a day or two we can make arrangements for you two to trade places. One of us will call the phone I gave you when we get it all worked out. We'll ring once, wait two minutes and ring you again. Go into the bathroom, close the door and turn on the water in both the sink and the bathtub before you call back. Ryan sends his love, Chili's fine. Sophie's at the Penthouse spoiling her. Give her love to Tony. I need to go, love you."

With that, she was gone. I sat on the bench to go over what she said.

When I exited the fitting room, Tony suggested I buy the dress so it looked like our shopping trip was on the up and up. We stopped by a café. "Are you going to tell me what your friend said? You were quiet on the way here. Is everything okay?"

"I'm sorry. Amy said so much in such a short time I was reviewing it in my mind. I'll start by telling you Sophie's okay. Someone from Johnny's family roughed her up pretty good. That's why she hasn't come home."

He leaned forward. "How bad is she hurt?"

"I got the impression it wasn't bad but it bruised her face and she can't come home until she can cover it with makeup. Amy gave me a throwaway phone and a small pistol. They say it will only be a few more days."

Tony's face softened when he found out his girlfriend was okay. We ate fish and chips, drank a beer and rode home in a peaceful silence.

I slept all night.

CHAPTER 20

Tony pulled into the driveway. A guard jogged up, checked the back seat and the trunk, tapped on the car and motioned us to drive through the gate. "You said earlier you thought Dominic had cold eyes. The story is he had a wife and two sons. They were all killed. Stories float around with several different scenarios about what happened to them."

I turned toward him. "What *did* happen to them?"

"I don't know. Mom knows but she says it's one of those secrets that could get me killed so she never told me."

Dominic had children. It was all I could think about. I thought the kids might be the answer to everything. I didn't have access to a computer, or any other electronics. There wasn't even a radio in my room. The phone Amy gave me only sent and received calls and texts. I would have to let her and Ryan research it. I sent a message. The minute I pushed the send button I remembered Amy's warning. I wondered if I had just made a big enough mistake to get me killed.

It wasn't safe to leave the phone out. I turned it on silent and put it in a jacket pocket of a coat in the closet. I was a person obsessed. Every five minutes I went to check it. *Get a grip*, I told myself.

Rosa brought in a tray with hot chocolate and a brownie. I sat in front of the window that faced out back, ate, and watched the birds as I sipped my warm drink. My goal was to fool my mind into thinking I didn't care about the news I waited for.

Before I went to bed, I looked one more time. Still nothing appeared. I fell into a fitful sleep only to be awakened by the morning sun as it streamed through the window. For a second, I forgot where I was. Once I acclimated to the light, I jumped up and raced to the closet to check the phone.

My answer appeared on the screen. Sophia knew there were two boys who would have been two, and three years older than she. She never saw or heard about them except through rumors over the years. She didn't know who their mother was.

I was about to write back when Rosa knocked and came in. She carried a dress in her arms. "Your father requests you accompany him to an anniversary party tonight for one of the elders of the Lombardi family. Johnny will be there. He wants you to wear this dress and low heel shoes. Be ready and downstairs by six."

She didn't stay. She laid the dress on the bed, smiled and left.

I hoped I wouldn't have to interact with Dominic or Johnny again before Sophie and I were back where we belonged— so much for hope.

I took a long hot shower and mulled over the guidelines Tony had given me. I brushed my teeth; put my make up on, and some other menial chores, all with my left hand. It was exhausting and infuriating.

A few minutes before six, I greeted Randle at the bottom of the stairs. He smiled. "Miss Sophia, you look lovely. Your father is in the car." He put my arm on his elbow and escorted me out.

My father said nothing until we arrived at the restaurant. "You look very presentable. Sit next to Johnny."

I was surprised when it was Tony who opened my door and led me to the entrance. He didn't speak or act as though he knew who I was. The family had strange rules.

Dominic sat at one end of the table. A man who reminded me of a boxer who'd been hit too many times stood behind him. The expensive clothes and haircut had done did nothing to soften his look.

Johnny was seated at the opposite end. He stood and came over to get me. He kissed me on the cheek. "You look lovely."

I muttered a thank you and let him lead me to my seat. A man followed me and stood near me, I guessed he was my protection.

Twenty-four people were seated at the main table, eight on each side and four at each end. The guests of honor were seated in the middle of one side. Someone tapped on a glass and noise erupted from all sides.

We ate salads, pasta, and warm bread. There were at least ten different sauces and noodles. It blew my theory that all noodles tasted the same and the sauce was the only thing that needed to vary.

Dominic stood and raised his wine glass. The room quieted. "I'd like to propose a toast to Samuel and Marie on their sixtieth wedding anniversary. Everyone held a glass in the air to honor the couple. Waiters carried in a large cake with a bride, groom, and a sixty on the top of it. They cut it and passed pieces around.

They brought out a small cake and sat it in front of the happy couple. Johnny leaned my way. "I need to excuse myself. I'll be right back. Enjoy your cake." I smiled at him before he left.

There was a commotion. I looked up in time to see Samuel's head as it fell into the cake in front of him. The guard behind me leaned down and said, "Let's go." I was in shock. He took my arm and hurried me along, "Now, Miss Sophia."

Father and his man were gone. I saw the tail lights of the car we arrived in as it turned the corner and sped away. A limousine pulled beside me in a matter of seconds. The man with me opened the door and shoved me in. He stuck his head into the passenger side window. "Take Miss Sophia home and use route C."

"Yes, Sir." And we were on our way.

"Tony, what happened?"

"I'm not sure what happened to Samuel, but I know Johnny's dead on the bathroom floor with a bullet in the back of his head."

"Who do you think killed him?"

"Dominic"

"Why would he, Tony? After he kidnapped me, made me come here, and planned a wedding to stop a war?"

"I think Johnny had Samuel killed so none of the older leaders would be around to speak against him as Don. He didn't have the support of the organization to become the Godfather. He's a disgusting man. No one liked him."

"So Dominic shot him?"

"He ordered it. Dominic would never get his hands dirty."

"Where're you going?"

"I'm taking route C. There are several routes mapped out by the *organization*. They either have fewer stop lights, fewer places to be ambushed, or some other trait to make it a safer ride. I don't know how long it'll take them to regroup and pick a leader. Once they do there'll be an all-out war. Those can last anywhere from a month to years."

I looked behind us. "I certainly don't want to be here and there's no way we'll bring Sophie here either."

"I agree. We need to stay out of sight and out of mind for the next twenty-four hours."

I couldn't believe I was so nervous. "What's going to happen?"

"All of the men will move to a location where they'll have a better advantage. There are only the two of you who are De Marcos, or at least are supposed to be family. We'll wait and see where your father wants you to go."

We pulled into the driveway, but no one was on the wall or in the guard house. The gate was locked. Tony got out, pushed some buttons and the gate opened. Once we were inside, he did the same thing.

"Go to your room and stay there."

I did as I was told.

CHAPTER 21

A commotion awoke me in the wee hours of the morning. I opened the bedroom door to look out. It was ghostly quiet in the house. I ran to the bedroom window.

The men packed cars with hundreds of guns and loads of food. It looked as if everyone was out there to help. Dominic and Tony were consciously missing. One by one the cars pulled out of the driveway. No guards manned the gate to check. Dominic came out at the last minute, surrounded by bodyguards armed with automatic weapons.

I went back to the hallway and looked out. It was eerily still. I took the gun Amy gave me and tucked it in the waistband of my slacks.

I walked through the dining room and left by a rear door I hadn't seen before. A hall led to a red door on the far side. I stood and listened. No one was in there. I went in.

I had found Dominic's private apartment. Nothing appeared to be old or outdated in his part of the house. My feet sank into the thick white carpet. Under more pleasant circumstances I would have taken off my shoes and let my feet slide around in the luxury.

The apartment consisted of two bedrooms, two baths, a sitting room, and a full kitchen with a private balcony off the kitchen door. It had comfy chairs and a state of the art barbeque grill with four tiers and two burners on each side.

Three unscalable stone walls boxed it in. Did Dominic cook? I couldn't muster up a picture in my mind of Dominic with an apron, a beer, and hamburgers on the grill. It struck me as so funny, I chuckled aloud.

Nothing looked out of place. I went back the way I came. The quiet unnerved me. I looked around the rest of the downstairs. As I walked upstairs, I heard a noise, ran to the huge landing, lay down, and made myself as small as possible.

The sound of heavy footsteps made my heart jump. They sounded as if they went toward the kitchen. When I thought the person was out of the room, I took off my shoes, and raced back to Sophie's room and shut the door. My heart pounded so hard I thought I would faint.

I crept through the bathroom to the closet and locked myself in.

My legs began to cramp. I was about to step out when the bedroom door opened. "Miss Sophie." Quieter. "Miss Sophia, are you here?" Footsteps pounded across the room as the man searched it...

I tried to push myself into the wall and not breathe.

"Kate?' Kate? Are you in there?"

I exhaled the breath I'd held. It was Tony. "Thank goodness, I didn't think you were coming back." I unlocked the door. "Where've you been? You didn't go with Dominic?"

He smiled at me. "One question at a time, I was outside getting my orders from Dominic. I'm supposed to deliver you to his aunt's in Manhattan until I can get you out of the country. One of Mother's friends took her to her sister's house in Queens. She forgot her passport. I took it to her. I want her out of harm's way. No one can predict what'll happen now."

I considered running. I watched out the window. The back appeared abandoned. I stormed across the room to the front. The same held true.

Tony hadn't been anywhere near the cars. It was about thirty-five miles from Newark to Queens. I didn't think he had been gone long enough to drive there and back.

I sat on the floor and leaned against the bed. "Let's call Amy and Ryan to come get us. If you're to take me to Manhattan, we could be miles away before they know we're missing."

He sat on the floor beside me. "Let me think a minute. This is one of those times I wish I was more of an insider. I know less about the big picture than most."

I put my hand on his arm. "I'm going to call them, unless you intend to stop me."

"I don't want to stop you; I don't want to spend the rest of my life looking over my shoulder either. Get one of them on the phone and let me talk to them. I know a place they can pick us up and no one can follow. While I give directions, put on something warm. It's a long and difficult hike."

I followed his direction. Twenty minutes later we scaled the back wall.

The farther we got from the lights of the compound, the thicker the brush became and the slower we moved. "I understand why you were so certain no one would follow us. I need to rest for a minute."

"It's not much farther. I'd say another half an hour and we'll be at the meeting spot."

I slumped to my knees to catch my breath. "I can't walk another step."

He sat on a rock facing me. "I could use a minute or two myself."

We rested in silence. Tony stood and reached down with both hands to help me up. "We'd better keep moving. It doesn't take long to get cold out here in the damp brush."

He pushed the twigs and small limbs out of my way as we creeped along. We came to a steep bank. At the top a gravel road stretched before us. "We're here."

A car flashed its lights and drove toward us.

Relief soared through me when Ryan and Amy got out. I hugged Ryan as if he was a lifeboat in the ocean during a storm. Amy wrapped her arms around the both of us. Tears of relief trickled down my face. I was safe.

Tony stood back. I let go of Ryan and walked to him. "This is Tony," I said to Ryan. "If it weren't for him, we might not have made it. Tony, this is Amy and Ryan."

Ryan stepped up and shook his hand. Amy hugged him. "I feel like I know you after talking to Sophie."

"I wish she was with you."

Ryan patted him on the back. "We do too. I didn't know if it was safe. You'll see her before the days over. I have a plane waiting. I thought you two might like to get away from this place."

Neither of us answered. We walked toward the car. I rode in front with Ryan.

He put his hand on my leg. "Bet you're tired and hungry."

Tony leaned forward. "I'm more nervous about getting out of here before someone sees us."

Ryan turned around and smiled. "I have it covered. We'll leave this car in a neighborhood between here and the airport. One of my men, Nathan, will pick us up. He does surveillance for a living. He'll know if anyone follows us. Our plane's in a hanger on the South end of the West runway. The main worry is will they try to find you and Sophia when all of this settles down?"

"Dominic told me to take Kate to Manhattan to his aunt's house. He thinks it's safe there. He'll be too busy to check for himself. I doubt if he gives her another thought. I'd say if we're careful we won't be missed."

I turned around and looked at him. "I hope you're right."

Four hours later we pulled up to the Penthouse.

When the elevator opened upstairs, there stood my twin sister. I still couldn't believe it. Tony walked over to her. They shared a loving hug.

She heaved a heavy sigh and looked over at me. "About two years ago your picture was in a magazine along with an article. I knew you were my sister, but I couldn't ask anyone for fear I would put you in danger or get myself killed. And now, here you stand, in front of me, in the same room. It's a dream come true."

She walked toward me with her arms out. We hugged and then I pushed her back so I could look at her face. "It is rather remarkable, after all these years of not knowing about each other, here we stand, together.

She smiled, pulled me to her again and gave me a bear hug. "I can't tell you how happy I am just to stand here, in the same room with you."

I took her hand and led her to the couch. Chili stood patiently on the arm waiting patiently to get a greeting. "Chili, I'm so glad to see you." She jumped down, ran around and jumped up to get Ryan to get her. I looked around, Amy, Ryan, Sophie, Tony, and Chili; my family.

"Do you have any idea why anyone would separate us at birth? And how you ended up with the Mafia and I with a woman who didn't think it was important enough to tell me? She swears she didn't know about you. I'll tell you Sophie, I've watched movies with worse plots than this."

We both laughed. I watched her as she absently petted Digger. Somehow I knew my sister would be an animal lover.

She met my gaze. "How did you like living with Dominic?"

I took Chili from Ryan. Digger had jumped from Sophie to Amy. "I don't know how you did it day after day. I found him intimidating when he didn't have to be and mean when he could have been kind."

Sophie moved to the love seat across from me. "I hope you don't mind. I would like to sit where I can see you. I would say you captured Dominic's persona perfectly."

"Denise or my mother, or whoever she, is treated me wonderfully. Since we found out about you and talked to her about my childhood, I have been dumbfounded. I don't have any idea what her motives were, but she was pretty much the perfect mother. It's what makes this such a mystery. Why? I believe I could get obsessed with it until I find out why."

Sophie looked at Tony and back to me. "I had three friendly people in my life, Tony, his mother, and for a few years, a lady named Roxy. Unless one of those three were with me, I was ignored. I would sit under Dominic's desk and color. He didn't acknowledge I was there. As I got older, I no longer fit under the desk."

Ryan asked, "What did you do then?"

She leaned forward as though what she was about to say was secret. "I pretended to study in his office as people came and went. I was mesmerized by what he did and said. Sometimes he said nothing. He merely pointed a finger or nodded his head and the things he wanted to be done were taken care of. I would run back to my room and write down everything I could remember; times, dates, names, and orders. I fantasized about Dominic leaving and me taking over as the new *capo di tutti capi*"

Amy had been sitting quietly in the lounge chair listening. "This is fascinating. Let's have a glass of wine."

Ryan got up. "Where are my manners? That sounds wonderful. Amy want to help me?"

They went to the other side of the bar and came back with glasses for everyone. Amy said, "I'm not savvy about Italian, Can you translate what you said earlier about capo..."

"Sure, it means *boss of all bosses.*

Amy sat her glass on the side table and picked up Digger who jumped at her feet for attention. "So you wanted your father dead?"

Sophie held her glass in one hand and covered her mouth with the other one. "I wasn't as sophisticated as that, but I believe there is a time in every child's life when they don't want to be held back by a parent who controls them. Dominic was worse than most."

I moved to sit with her and took her hand. "You don't still want to run the Mafia, do you? It seems so dangerous."

Tony sat on the other side of her and leaned forward so I could see him as he talked. "I was there. It was a childhood fantasy we played out whenever Dominic was unnecessarily mean or cruel to Sophie or anyone else. It eased the pressure. He even controlled the snacks she ate, the shoes and clothes she wore, and the way she wore her hair."

She took my hand in hers. "It was the childhood I had. I wouldn't want any kid to have to live like that. It would be a thousand times more treacherous for someone like you. I would venture to say I know as much about our family and the Lombardi as anyone else who might try to claim the position. I also have hundreds of notebooks that chronicle the visits, talks, persons, and plans of the De Marcos from the time I was eight years old until I left there off and on a couple of years ago. Once I let everyone know the information exists, no one will dare touch me."

I turned more squarely toward her. It wasn't my business. I needed to remember that. She had a life for over thirty years before she knew about me. I wanted to keep my voice clear, steady, and unconcerned. It didn't work. "Do you still want to take over?"

Tony smiled, "It isn't that easy. In America there has never been a woman run a family. There are a few in the big families in the old country, but not on this side of the ocean."

She put both of her hands on my knees. "I'm over it. I couldn't kill someone or order it done. I couldn't take money that was illegally obtained. What I'm going to do is write a *tell-all* book and get them all arrested."

"Even Dominic?"

"Especially Dominic."

We stopped our conversation to watch the nightly news. We were starved for information and the newspaper wouldn't arrive until morning.

We didn't have to wait long. The lead story captivated us ...

What is being called the first all out Mafia war since 1954, started Wednesday at the La Maida Italian Restaurant in Newark, New Jersey?

In a rare show of solidarity, Dominic De Marco and his daughter Sophia joined the Lombardi family to celebrate Samuel Lombardi's sixtieth wedding anniversary. After cake was served and as guests proposed toasts to the happy couple, Samuel collapsed. Until the findings of the autopsy are released, authorities say it was most likely a heart attack.

Johnny Lombardi, the Under Boss and next in line to be Don at Samuels death was found in a private bathroom with a gunshot wound to the back of his head. The FBI described to the shooting as execution style.

A rumor floated through both families that Johnny and Sophie De Marco were be married in less than a month.

Unnamed sources reported the union would have solidified the tenuous position Johnny held in his own family.

The next in line to head the family is Frank 'Knuckles' Anaton.

Ryan pressed the off button on the remote. With the sound from the TV silenced, the room was still. Sophie broke the spell. "Dominic made it a sure thing which family would run New Jersey. Frank Anton is ruthless, but not smart enough to be a Don."

I took the last sip of water in my glass. "How does it work? How do you decide who takes what position?"

Ryan went into the kitchen for wine and water to refill our drinks. "I've always been fascinated by organized crime, he said. I run up against it whenever I try to expand my business to the East coast. The biggest push back is from New Jersey."

Sophie explained. "The head is the Don, Boss, or Godfather. He must be a blood relative. Second in command is the Underboss. It's pretty much a given he'll be the next Boss. He must also be a blood relative."

Ryan put his hand up like we did in grade school. "Frank "Knuckles" Anaton doesn't sound like blood."

"He is, he's Samuel's nephew on his wife's side. Her maiden name was Lombardi."

"Your knowledge of the Mafia is truly amazing," Amy was impressed.

Sophie stood and smiled. "I didn't study it, Amy; I lived it nearly every day. If you all will excuse me, I'd like to go to my room. My head's spinning. I need to think. Tony, would you like to join me?"

I stood and walked to her. "You'll never know how happy I am to have you in my life. Had you not pursued it, I would have never known you existed. Thank you."

She kissed me on the cheek and pushed me an arm's length away. "Yes, I do know how happy you are. I feel the same way." She looked around the room to Amy and Ryan. "And to have friends like the two of you and Tony by my side, I'm blessed."

CHAPTER 22

Ryan went into the other room to make a few business calls. Amy and I shared a glass of wine and talked. "I feel as if I always see you yet we never talk." she said.

I raised my glass to her. "To you, and, me, and Nash Investigations. May we one day be able to do cases again."

"Wouldn't that be wonderful?" She set her glass down. "Kate, I need to talk to you about something."

The look on her face alarmed me. "Oh my, you aren't quitting are you?"

She ran her finger across the rim of her glass. "No, it's Jake. He's seeing someone in Springfield."

I put my hand on hers. "I'm so sorry. Tell me about it."

Tears streamed down her cheeks. She wiped them with the back of her hand. "He says he's lonely. He's only here a few days every month. I take off as much as I can when he's here, but sometimes we're in the middle of a case. I can't go to Springfield at the drop of a hat because he wants to go to dinner with some of the other players and their wives.

"He loves Digger here, but there, it's difficult. There are three of them in the house. They don't watch him when they go in and out. Sometimes they don't close the door at all. I'm a nervous wreck the entire time I'm there. Do I sound like it's all about the dog? It isn't, you know."

"I know it isn't about Digger, and Jake can take care of himself. The dog can't. If you want to try to fix this, we'll take Digger over here when you go to visit. Chili would love it."

"That's my other problem. Please don't tell Ryan what I'm about to share with you."

I put Chili on the floor, took Amy's glass and got us some more wine.

She picked up Digger and came to the counter. We sat across from one another. "Ok, I hope this doesn't sound horrible. Jake and I haven't progressed in seven years. Our relationship is the same as it was. He's thirty-seven. At that age, the chances of him going to the major league is slim to none.

"He might get traded among the Triple A Clubs. Most of the players get jobs and give it up at thirty-two. Jake has no interest in anything but baseball. We can be in the middle of a conversation and something about baseball will come on the TV or radio and he completely forgets I'm there."

She stopped, petted Digger, who walked across the counter to me, and reached down to get Chili who jumped to try to get her to pick her up. "Do you want to fix this with Jake?"

"That's what I'm getting too. Lately I have been spending a lot of time with Nathan. He's interested in everything. He gardens, cleans his own house, cooks, and can talk on any subject. I love it."

"You love it or him?" I asked.

"That's the difference between Jake and me. I wouldn't let anything happen between Nathan and me so long as he's in the picture. I don't even know if he's interested."

As if on cue, Ryan came around the corner. "He is."

The conversation came to an abrupt end. Amy's face was beet red. Ryan smiled. "I'm sorry I horned in. One of the calls I had to make was to Nathan. There's a family wedding next Saturday night and he wants to invite you. He's scared to death about it. He doesn't want to drive a wedge between you and Jake."

Amy put one hand on each cheek. "What a mess. What I wanted to tell you was that I think I'm going to stop seeing Jake. It has nothing to do with Nathan, the distance, the dog, the lack of commonality, and of course no matter what I say, the other woman, in my opinion, is unforgivable."

Ryan walked over to Amy and kissed her on the top of the head. "Did Nathan tell you about his high school girl-friend?"

Amy shook her head no.

"They dated all the way through high school but went their separate ways for college. Nathan saved money the en-tire time. He didn't date anyone else. He was in love. He bought her a ring he was going to give her after graduation.

"She had never hinted her feelings for him were differ-ent or that she had met someone else. When she came home they took up where they left off. To shorten this story; before he had the chance to ask her to marry him, she told him she was going to Cleveland to meet her new boyfriend's parents before they became engaged.

"Nathan hasn't dated much since then. He's a super guy. He's your age, but not date savvy. If you decide to date him, go slow. Don't break his heart."

He took Chili from me. "I'll leave you two to talk. My girlfriend and I are going for a walk. Want me to take Digger along?"

"Sure, he would like that."

I turned my attention to Amy. "What will you do?"

"After all these years; he would do something like that makes me wonder what else he has done. I don't want to get out of one relationship and jump into another. Nathan and I are good friends. I hope he asks me to the wedding. I'd like to stay on the friendship path with him for a long while."

I walked around the counter and hugged her. I loved her. She had been my friend and partner for years. I wanted to see her happy.

We sat and finished our wine in a comfortable silence only true friends understand. When Ryan came back with the dogs, she went home.

I got ready for bed and waited for Ryan. He had more calls to make.

His first words, when he came in the room were. "Why did Amy go home?"

"When life doesn't go your way, home is your safe place. I hate what happened. She would've been fine to break up with Jake, but for him to move on without letting her know was rotten."

He walked over and hugged me. "You won't do that to me will you?"

"Ryan, I don't have the time or energy to have an affair."

I picked Chili up and put her next to me on the bed. He Ryan laid down, turned on his side toward me, put his elbow on the bed, and rested his chin on his hand. "Did they treat you badly in New Jersey?"

I petted the dog. "I wouldn't say badly. It was nerve-wracking to pretend to be someone else. She uses the opposite hand, has an accent I wasn't sure I could mimic, and Dominic is overbearing and cold."

He reached over, pushed my hair away from my face and kissed me gently. "I love you, Kate. I would like to make a life-time commitment to you."

I didn't often get overwhelmed. My take-a-step-back-and-breathe method usually worked. It didn't work this time. My head pounded and sweat ran down my face and pooled on my neck. I'd never had a panic attack, but it was that or malaria.

Ryan must have sensed my distress he went into the bathroom and came back with a wet rag. He put it on my forehead. "Relax; it isn't every week you interact with a person who orders people killed. A sister who you didn't know about for thirty-four years, a partner who breaks up with her guy after years together and a boyfriend who wants you to move out of your safe place and marry him. Let's forget it for tonight. I'll ask again at a more appropriate time."

CHAPTER 23

I woke to thunder and lightning. Heavy rain hammered the roof. I never liked storms with high wind, but I loved to watch the lightning and listen to thunder.

Ryan and Chili were gone. It was after eight. I hoped they had their walk before the rain. I didn't hear anything in the living area so I took a shower, put on some comfy clothes, my fluffy bedroom slippers, and padded to the kitchen to make a cup of latte. Sophie sat on the love seat staring out at the storm.

I made my drink, went in, and sat beside her. She put her hand on mine. "Do you believe this?"

"It's difficult. I'm glad to have a sister, and a twin is a plus, but I can't help but wonder if there's some secret that can destroy our lives."

She stood and walked closer to the balcony door. "I don't think there is. Dominic's a self-absorbed, self-centered, narcissistic, and evil man. The only reason he does anything is to advance his own agenda. He would have married me off to a nasty man almost twice my age. I'm convinced the reason he shot Johnny was because something changed and having Johnny dead turned the situation to his advantage."

"You really hate him. When he thought I was you, he indicated the marriage would be temporary."

"Hate is a strong word. Let's say I wouldn't waste tears over him if I never saw him again, and he would say or do anything to get what he wanted."

Tony walked in. He looked different. I'd only seen him in a suit and tie. He had on a muted orange Polo shirt, khaki pants, and loafers. He didn't have his usual slicked back hair. It was dry, unruly and attractive. He looked much younger. "Hi ladies, any plans for the day?"

Sophie looked at me. "I'd like to research the hospital and the De Marco family history. There are some things we know are true. We have the same mother and father, and our birth certificates were signed by the same people. "

"Working in investigation so long, I know there is always someone willing to tell the story. We need to find them. I do have information about Dr. Signorelli, Denise's background, and our *so-called* mother, Julie Lombardi."

Tony got a cup of coffee and walked back to the couch. He turned on the TV along the way.

A picture of Dominic stared back at us as we listened to the anchorman. *Mob boss, Dominic De Marco, and two associates were killed in a fiery car crash on the GWB. Witnesses say the car was traveling at a speed of over one hundred miles an hour. The car exploded which damaged the guardrail. The driver lost control of the 2016 Cadillac. It went airborne and landed in the cold waters below. Divers are searching for the bodies.*

Traffic on three lanes on the upper deck was closed and two on the lower deck due to debris. Authorities say traffic will have to be routed around the damaged lanes for several months.

Sophie got up and walked toward the kitchen. "Isn't it convenient the bodies went into the deep waters?"

I followed her. "You think the story's not true?"

She stopped to put cream in her coffee. "Oh, I believe three poor souls perished in the accident. I would bet everything I have that none of them was Dominic. Unfortunately, it was three people he thought were expendable. He was good at deciding who was good enough to live and who wasn't."

I reached for a K-cup when she stepped away from the counter. "Is he that ruthless?"

She gave me a flat-eyed stare. "To run a mob family one has to be cutthroat. I'm sure his father before him taught him the ends justify the means."

Tony laughed. "I don't want this to sound sexist but I'm glad a woman has never taken over a Mafia crime family."

Sophia walked over and looked out the window. "If he faked his own death it was because he knew he was about to be arrested, or someone threatened to kill him and he believed they could do it."

I had gone closer so I could hear her. "So, you think he faked it?"

Tony joined us. "It doesn't matter. Once they declared it was him, whether it was or not, he can't come back. We haven't been there. We don't know if the walls were closing in on him or not."

"As a child, I daydreamed about what I could do with all that money. It's a vast fortune. While he was alive, he had control, but on his death it automatically transfers to me. He couldn't take too much money or everyone would know he's around and never stop looking for him. He kept a couple of million dollars in a safe in his room."

"I went to his apartment and looked around. All of his personal things were there, even cufflinks."

"The safe's built into the floor under his dresser. I don't know if you noticed, but it would take at least three men to move it."

I was intrigued. "How could he get in it without help?"

"The back slides up. Once he moves it, he can access it from the bottom drawer. He carries the key in his pocket."

Tony clasped his hands behind his head. "I doubt if he could move more than two million. One million weighs twenty-two pounds if it is in hundred dollar bills. He's either leaving the country or having a new identity fabricated."

"How do you know what one million dollars weights off the top of your head?"

Tony looked at Sophie for what looked like a signal as to whether he should proceed with his opinions. She smiled and nodded her head. "Without going into great detail about Mafia hierarchy, the soldiers, mostly hired thugs enforce the rules. They beat, kidnap, or kill whoever they have to in order to make sure the business owners and drug dealers give them the money they went to collect. They don't take anything but cash. Each group has a Capa over them. The Capas handle nearly all of the money."

Sophie shook her head. "It wasn't unusual for fifty to a hundred thousand dollars to come in each week. Except for a select few, everyone was paid in cash."

"How does it get from cash to the bank without someone questioning it?"

Apparently Tony enjoyed his job as teacher. "They used crooked bankers, lawyers who set up Delaware corporations and through the trash company, rental buildings, and the fruit warehouse downtown, all businesses owned by De Marco Enterprises."

Chili jumped on my lap. Ryan stood behind me. We were too engrossed in the conversation to hear him come in. "Hi, you were gone a long time."

"It doesn't appear anyone missed me."

"Sure we did. Have you heard the national news?"

"Yes, what happens now?"

"I'll catch you up later. As knowledgeable as you are about organized crime, you probably know anyway."

"Dominic signed everything over to me when I was eighteen. If he was arrested, he didn't want to lose it due to the forfeiture laws."

Ryan sat next to me. We all four settled on the couch and love seat. Chili was busy taking her toy from person to person to have them toss it so she could retrieve it.

Ryan inquired. "I bet you weren't prepared for this, Sophie. Any idea what you will do?"

She sat across from me. "Yes, I would sell the mansion, liquidate the holdings, take all the money and set up a foundation. I can't undo all of the horrible things Dominic De Marco did, but I can try to help more people than he destroyed."

I heard my stomach growl. "My belly is reminding me we haven't eaten. Anyone hungry?"

We headed for the kitchen. I pulled sandwich items from the refrigerator and set them on the counter. It might have been a little early for lunch, but no one complained. The food must have perked everyone up because the conversation flowed. I filled Ryan in on the parts he missed.

We ate at the bar. "I don't know whether to give you my condolences or congratulations.

While I was out I went by the office and got these." He handed each of them a card. "They say Meade Enterprises on them. You only need to show this for identification." He handed them another card and laid two envelopes on the table. "Each of these has money in it. Use what you need. If you run out, let me know."

Sophie smiled. "It seems funny for us to take anything from you since we're sitting on hundreds of millions of dollars."

Tony added. "Thank you. It might be awhile before we get any money. At least until we find out what's going on and if any of the organization is intact. We'll pay you back."

Ryan stood. "It's no big deal. I'm an optimist. I'm sure something wonderful will come out of this."

Amy called to say Jake was in town and his afternoon game had been canceled. She wanted to take the day off to straighten things out between them. Who was I to say no to someone who had been doing all of the work?

I longed to get back to private investigations and my life. It wasn't going to happen anytime soon if we didn't figure out the mystery that was us.

We were no closer on day one than on day three. Tony and Sophie let us know their concerns. "I'm restless without any information from home. By now everyone knows Tony and I are missing. If I don't show up there soon, other lawyers will get involved and muddy the waters."

Amy showed up the next morning, she looked like she had been crying. I couldn't get her alone long enough to ask her about it.

She, like the rest of us, was frustrated by the lack of progress on our real identities. "The biggest problem we have is that the Mafia, Cosa Nostra, and Dominic, nor any of his family has a Facebook page. Let's face it. The entire world is online. Our information is in cyberspace; theirs isn't."

Ryan laid a booklet on the table. "This is something Neil, my tech guy, came up with. It's how to find anyone using the internet, even if our subject doesn't use it." He looked at me and Amy. "I know you have found hundreds of lost children, wayward husbands, and runaway wives over the years. The reason we haven't tried the same procedures you use in the office is because it's too personal."

We all agreed. Neil's resources were the same as we always used. What we needed to do was make a list of everything we all knew about the Mafia of New Jersey, my mother, Honor Hospital, our lives, Dominic's life and on and on. The key was to stop making it complicated and use buzz *words*.

I put my feet on the couch."Buzzwords are a good idea."

For the next ten minutes we gave every word we could. Ryan put them down on his cell phone and sent them to Neil.

Ryan stood. "Let's get out of here for awhile. Anyone like ice cream?"

Sophie and I said, "I do," at the same time.

We drove to Ted Drew's and ordered decadent treats. It was an unseasonably warm night, so we sat on the curb like little kids.

Ryan handed Sophie a banana split. "Did you get much ice cream as a kid, Sophie?

She looked from one of us to another, stopped when she got to Tony and laughed. "No, nothing was normal or common about my life. When I left for college they sent Tony to protect me. It was equivalent to sending a fox to guard the henhouse.

"To give you an example of my childhood, Dominic agreed to let me try out for the senior play in High School. We put on Peter Pan and I was Tinkerbelle. It meant practice every evening after school. One of his men sat in the back row of the theater every night to watch me. It was dark back there and hardly anyone noticed him.

"I loved it, the freedom and the action—until opening night. Here came my father with three SUV's, six armed bodyguards, and the biggest bouquet ever put together. He held it all evening.

"Hardly anyone watched the play. They stared at Dominic, the flowers, and the guards. I was humiliated. The students, who worked hard for months, were angry. When I didn't think it could get any worse, his cell phone rang in the middle of the last act. He left before the end of the play. I didn't get the flowers."

Amy put her hands up to cover her mouth. "That's awful. What did you do?"

"I laughed. I saw the irony of it. It was ludicrous. "

We sat for awhile longer and talked about Ryan's work and why I became a detective. By the time we left, we were tired, stuffed, and ready to settle in.

Amy and I stayed outside the Penthouse and talked about our business. We decided to take another case to keep the cash flowing. Since my brain whirled around the events of the last two weeks, we agreed she would pick one.

Tony and Sophie were in their room when I got off the elevator. Ryan sat on the couch and grinned at me. He patted the cushion next to him. "I have a present for you. It's something I've wanted to give you for weeks." He reached into his jacket pocket and took out a thick heavy envelope.

"What is this?"

"Look at it and you'll know. I don't want to spoil the surprise after all this time."

I had butterflies. I took it in both hands and turned it over twice. There were folded papers inside. They looked like legal documents. I opened it and freed its contents Ryan *Russell Meade, and Kathleen Madison Nash, joint tenants with right of survivorship.* "Ryan, I don't know what to say. You bought our *arrest* house."

"I did. We loved it before that horrible ordeal took place. I made an offer and they took it. We are proud homeowners."

"I'm embarrassed. Do you think they'll remember us and what happened?"

He took the papers, laid them on the table and pulled me to him. I snuggled my head against his cheek. "Even if they remember, an evening with you and they'll realize it didn't make a difference. There were three homes for sale on Lafon Place when we looked at that one. It was the only one left. I couldn't let it get away. Houses changing hands in that neighborhood is rare. How many couples can say they were arrested outside their home before they owned it?"

"I haven't had time to think about it, but now that we have it, I'm excited. Tell me there is no need to move right away. You haven't rented this apartment out have you?"

"Before it's officially ours, you'll have to go to the Title Company and sign the papers. And no, I thought if Sophia and Tony stayed in St. Louis, they could live in it until they decided what to do with their new lives'"

Chili had been asleep on the floor at Ryan's feet. She jumped up, ran to the elevator and barked. Ryan scooped her up. "I'll take her."

"Are you spoiling her? She just came in, but it's a gorgeous night, I'll go with you."

CHAPTER 24

I put on a jacket and got my Glock. I wore it so much I was naked without it. Ryan had Chili's lead. The night air was a bit cooler than earlier, Chili loved it. Ryan let her stop and smell every bush and light post.

She did her business in front of a *keep the city clean can.* They were wonderful. Each held a little bag to pick up after your canine and a trash receptacle to dispose of it.

I jumped when a man I hadn't seen coming, yelled at me. "Sophia. It would be best if you stopped searching for answers and let sleeping dogs lie."

He had gotten out of the black SUV like the ones at the Compound. Ryan shielded the dog in his arms and stepped in front of me. "Who are you? Who sent you?"

The man didn't answer; he walked to the far side of the car and got in. The driver put his window down. "Some people care what happens to you, Miss Sophie. The only way to stay safe is to let the past go and build a future."

They drove off. The car had no plates or identifying characteristics. We turned toward home. "What do you think of that?"

Ryan put Chili on the ground. "The gist of it was they'll leave Sophie alone if she lets her past go and focuses on the future."

"That's pretty much what I thought. It also tells me Dominic is alive and well."

I would have told Sophie and Tony what happened, but when we got back they were still in the bedroom with the door shut. It could wait until later.

Chili danced around the floor, turning in circles to beg for treats. Ryan indulged her.

"If you give her a treat every time she does something cute, her belly will drag the ground and we'll have to put her on a skateboard and pull her around."

He picked her up. "Did you hear what she said about your figure? She said you would get fat. I bet you're not over eight pounds."

We laughed.

These days of intrigue and mystery wore me out. I got ready for bed and snuggled with the dog as I waited for Ryan. I must have fallen asleep. When I awoke, the sun shined through the bedroom window. I went to the kitchen area. Tony had cut bananas, strawberries, oranges, and grapefruit. The platter was beautiful. "You have an eye for that."

He looked up and presented the tray to me so I could choose something. "I helped my mom cater dinners at the Compound on many occasions. There's no doubt in my mind I could pull off a four-course meal without a hitch." He grinned at me.

"Good to know. Ryan can cook better than me."

Sophie sat on a stool. "I have never cooked a thing in my life."

We ate and laughed. I had never had family other than Michael and my mom. It made me happy all the way to my toes to have a sister.

As we cleaned up our mess, Ryan's phone rang. He put his hand over the microphone. "It's Neil. He has our results. He emailed them to me."

He opened his laptop and read. *Denise Madison died in a drowning accident on Table Rock Lake on the Fourth of July, 1970. She reappeared in June of 1978 and taught at Frances Howell High School in St. Peters.*

Dominic De Marco married Jane Dancing De Marco on September 23; 1964.They had two children, Daniel and Jeffrey. The boys were killed along with their mother in an automobile accident in October 1979. The boys were six and nine. The authorities could never rule out foul play. It was thought a rivalry between the De Marco Crime Family and the Lombardi Family contributed to the accident.

Dominic had two sisters and two brothers. His oldest sister, Louisa disappeared in June of 1978 and was never found. His sister, Margaret, was murdered by the mob in 1988. His brother Frank was gunned down while at the horse races. His brother Michael died of a fever in 1962.

There has never been a nurse licensed as Sally Jeffers. There were three Sally Jeffers in that time period, in the St. Louis area; one was a housekeeper at Honor Hospital, one an airline flight attendant and number three was a family attorney.

There were four Dr. A. Signorelli's in the greater St Louis area. One died in 1954, one was a dentist and died in 1979. One moved to work at the Mayo Clinic in March of 1978 and the last one died in a skydiving accident in 1977.

Honor Hospital was founded in April of 1950 and was bought and revamped as a rehabilitation center in 1983. The CEO was Martin Aldo. Head of surgery was Silas Green.

"That's a lot of information. He says if he finds anything else important, he'll send it."

Ryan's email alert dinged again. "This is interesting, when Neil put the names Kathryn Ann Madison and Sophia Lynn De Marco in the search engine together, he got nothing. When he accessed the *dark web*; this is what came up.

Born: Missouri Baptist Hospital, April 1, 1980, Mother:
Margaret De Marco, Father: Jonathan Gaddu. Baby
Kathryn was born first at 1:36 am and Sophia at 1:45 am."

The room was so still all I heard was breathing.

Ryan came over to me. "Do you still have that board we
used to play Pictionary? It had paper attached and we used it
to draw on. I'd like to make a family tree and timeline."

"Sure, all that stuff's in here. We all had such a good
time with it; I couldn't bear to throw it away." I smiled at
them while I dug for the old toy.

Ryan stood beside the board. "Let's make a timeline,
and who's who. I'm sure we all caught the dates, but let's be
sure."

I sat down on the couch and looked at the emails.
"Okay, Denise Madison died July 1974 but reappeared June
1978."

Sophie leaned over the back of the couch so she could
read over my shoulder. "Louisa, Dominic's older sister disappeared a month after Denise reappeared. Denise was never
seen again, and you saw Denise Madison a few weeks ago.
Do you think they are the same person?"

Tony joined the conversation. "If Denise Madison, your
adopted Mother and Louisa De Marco are one in the same,
your supposed mother would be your aunt and Dominic
would be your uncle."

"It gets more complicated than that, our mother is another De Marco I've never heard of before, Margaret. She
was executed by the mob in 1988. And who's Jonathan Gaddu? How did another hospital become involved and why
have we been a secret so long?"

Ryan called for quiet. "Let's get this chart made so we
can study the players."

I continued down the facts we had. "Brother Frank was
gunned down at the Horse Races. Sounds like another mob
hit. It says we were born at Missouri Baptist Hospital in St
Louis. I have some facts about Jonathan. It says Jonathan
Gaddu, New York Stage Producer. He won more Tony

awards(21) for his achievements than any producer of his
time, three for Best Musical, eight for Best Producer, six for
his directing, and four special awards.

He was married to Margaret De Marco in June of 1973.
It gives his birth date as August 7, 1944. It says related arti-
cles—The Mafia murder of Mickey *the lip* Amato."

Ryan agreed he would look the article up while I took
Chili out and fed her. When I came back I was invigorated
by the fresh air and ready to know more about my life.

The phone rang. "Hi, Amy, what's up? Really? No kidding? Well, bring it and Nathan and come on over." I hung
up. "Amy says she and Nathan watched a movie last night
and we need to watch it. I told her to come on over."

No one spoke a word. Ryan paraphrased the article.
"Mickey 'the lip' Amato was out on bail. He had Rico
charges pending and two murder indictments. He must have
been up to no good because as he sat in his limousine, outside the Fox Theater, six gangsters from another crime family tried to ambush him before he could appear in court the
following day.

"Mrs. Gaddu, (Sister of New Jersey crime boss Dominic
De Marco) waited for her husband (the famous New York
Theater mogul, Jonathon Gaddu) in her chaffered rental car,
behind him.

"When Amato realized it was a hit, He stepped out of
his car with a machine gun and preceded to kill all six men
who had come to do him harm. Margaret Gaddu's driver left
the scene as quickly as possible, but not fast enough.

"On March 31, 1980, Amato and his henchmen followed
the car and murdered the driver and Gaddu's nine-month
pregnant wife in the middle of Kingshighway Boulevard.
The driver was pronounced at the scene and Mrs. Gaddu was
pronounced dead later at Honor Hospital along with her un-
born baby.

Mickey Amato was to be arraigned in federal court in
downtown St. Louis on April 2, 1980. He was under heavy

guard, yet a sniper's bullet found both he and his co-defendant, Sammy *little man* Gusto as they left the court.

"No one was charged with the murder but it has always been thought that Dominic De Marco, was responsible as revenge for his sister's death."

CHAPTER 25

O nce Amy and Nathan arrived we got comfortable and watched the movie. The first five minutes were horrible. Some giant cricket chased people, grabbed them and held them in his legs while he dined on them.

I asked. "Is this a joke?"

Nathan held up a hand. "Wait, we're almost to the good part."

A minute or two later, a small red-headed woman, ran down a street against the crowd. When she got to the person she wanted, she turned around. Sophie and I gasped. It was us, or enough of a likeness to know we were related. We watched closely. She was the star and she and her male co-star electrocuted the beast and went off to live happily ever after.

Ryan slowed the film down so we could more easily read the credits. The woman who looked like us was Roxy Watkins.

Sophie put both hands up to her mouth. "Tony! Do you recognize her?"

"Yes. She was the woman who came to play with you a few times a week. When you were eight, we never saw her again. You cried for her every day for weeks. Do you remember her?"

"Yes. She was sweet and loving; there wasn't much of that in my childhood. After she didn't come for a week or so, Dominic came to my room. He had never been there before, nor did he ever come again. I remember word for word what he said me. *Sophia, come closer, I want to talk to you. Your friend can not come to see you anymore. She wanted me to tell you she wishes she could, and she loves you more than you will ever know.*"

Tony said, "Now we know why—Roxy Watkins was Margaret De Marco. He must have cared about his sister. She was gunned down in 1988. It explains a lot. Why she changed her name, why she didn't take you two to raise? What I don't understand is why they didn't have both of you at the estate.''

I interjected. "I don't know how they faked her death from a gunshot wound the first time? And how was it we were born at a different hospital?"

Ryan picked Chili up and said. "Why don't we leave it until tomorrow? I'm on information overload. Nathan, can I borrow the movie so I can take it over to Neil and get a copy?"

"I already did, boss. The copy we watched is yours."

Nathan and Amy left. The four of us sat in silence for a few minutes until I confessed. "I need some time alone to go over all of this in my head."

"I like to do that too," Sophie said. "We'll see you in the morning.

CHAPTER 26

I took a hot shower and put on clean clothes. Ryan and Chili had been gone for hours. I didn't know if I should have been worried or not.

My phone was in the living room. I went to get it. Sophie sat alone on the couch. "Where's Tony?"

"He went for a walk. He's been gone a long time."

"Not good. Last night Ryan and I took the dog out. Two men in a black SUV gave us a warning to stop investigating our past and live in the present if we wanted to be left alone. Ryan has been gone for hours. I had best go after them."

"Didn't you think that might be something we would want to know?"

"Yes, absolutely. You were asleep when we came in. This morning I forgot. I guess Ryan did too. I had better go look for them. Is Tony armed?"

"Yes, want me to go along."

"No. Stay here and be safe. Tony might need to get in. If he does, it's important to check the camera to make sure no one is trying to use him as a cover to get up here."

I walked into my room, picked up my Glock and put it in my pants near the small of my back. I put another clip in my jacket pocket. On the way down, I called Ryan's cell, he didn't answer.

I stayed off the sidewalk and stepped lightly into the shadows of the building. Ryan's truck was parked another block down on the other side of the street. A wave of fear soared through me. Not only was Ryan out, but he had the puppy with him. I was sick with worry.

I wanted to go to the truck to see if Chili was in it. I leaned against the cool brick of the building and sized up my options. The vehicle sat twenty yards from me. If I went over to it, I wouldn't have any cover.

I heard a scuffle ahead of me. I walked toward it. Tony was on the ground. Ryan knelt beside him, gun drawn. Two men stood over both of them. They also held guns. It looked like a standoff.

I moved close enough to listen. Ryan spoke to one of the men. "This man has no interest in you or your business. He wants to go on with his life. He has no intention of causing trouble for anyone."

The other one kicked Tony's leg. "How do you know what he wants? He knows too much."

I worked my way behind them. Ryan saw me but didn't move or flinch. He went on with the drama in front of him. "There were two men here last night with the same message. Tony and Sophia want to have a family and a life. They intend to move far away. They don't want to hurt anyone."

When I was a foot behind the men, I stuck my Glock in one man's left's ear. "Put your guns on the ground and kick them toward him." I pushed him toward Ryan, and forced my weapon further into his ear.

Ryan scrambled to his feet. "You heard her. Drop your weapons."

Both men bent slightly to put the guns on the sidewalk. I frisked the man on the left and the gunman on the right. The first man had a second shoulder holster on the other side.

The other one had a knife with a ten-inch blade in his boot. These men were serious. "I got here late to the party; you'll have to tell me what this is about."

Ryan challenged them. "If I have this correct, they would like to take Tony and Sophia as a bargaining chip to get what control they can of the De Marco crime family. Is that right, gentlemen?"

"We represent the De Marcos," one of them boasted.

Tony opened his eyes and scrambled to his feet. "You guys don't know much, do you? Dominic wouldn't sacrifice anything to save Sophia. And you are not from the *family.*"

They looked at one another and whispered a couple of things. "We were hired by a guy from the city to find the De Marco woman and take her back to him. Something about her ole man."

Tony stood as close as he could to the speaker. "The only thing that can happen here is that you end up dead. I'm going to tell you this one time. Don't come around here again. You don't know enough about the people you want to scam. The only outcome here would be your funerals. You aren't from the De Marco family, but I am. You don't want to mess with any of us."

I picked their guns up one at a time, broke them down, and scattered the parts in every direction. The man's second gun, I stuck in my waistband and I handed the knife to Ryan. I stood on my tiptoes so I was even with the guy's nose. "Are we done here?"

Neither one answered. They got in the car and left.

I walked toward Ryan's truck. "Where's my dog?"

Ryan laughed. "I knew it. You didn't come for me. You came because you were worried about Chili. She's locked in the truck."

I ran over to get her. I heard Ryan press the electronic lock as I got closer so I could get in.

"Let's go home," I suggested to all of them.

Once we were safe in the apartment we turned on cable news. The headline was—...*the body of Dominic De Marco and two unidentified males were pulled from the Hudson River early today. The bodies were badly decomposed but De Marco was positively identified by family, close friends, identifying marks, and tattoos. Arrangements will be announced later.*

Tony slipped off his jacket and sat on the couch. "Isn't that convenient, once the bodies were too decomposed to identify, they are recovered. Dominic and a few million dollars are somewhere on an island laughing at everyone."

Sophie sat beside him. "Why would he leave? He was the Boss, the Don, everyone did as he said. What would change that?"

"It's one of the secrets they don't want us to learn," Ryan stated.

CHAPTER 27

Ryan suggested we visit Mother once again. Sophie and I wanted to find Jonathon Gaddu. If he was truly our father, he could tell us about Roxy Watkins or Margaret De Marco or both.

We all sat on the balcony, in the sun, and enjoyed the fresh air. I walked to the railing and turned to face them. "Sophie and I are going to fly to New York and visit Mr. Gaddu. We believe, if he is our father, he can shed light on the mystery surrounding us."

Tony and Ryan looked at one another. Tony stood. "I am going to stay here, go to Missouri Baptist Hospital and see if I can expand on the information we have."

Ryan glanced at Tony. I had the feeling they had discussed not going with us. "I haven't put in a full day of work in over a month. I'll stay here with Tony. That way, neither one of us has to eat dinner alone."

Ryan made our reservation. We would fly out in the afternoon. When I went to pack, my sister followed me. "I don't have any clothes of my own so I'm going to have to wear yours again. I know I should buy some. I haven't wanted to go out. I had a suitcase with me, but it got lost somewhere."

I pointed to the closet. "Take what you need. Sorry it's such a mess. I have expectations of cleaning it, but there's always something pressing that keeps me from it. Yours was so neat and organized."

She picked out a dress, some slacks and tops. "I have a maid. I'm not sure it was a great loss. They might have had a tracker in it. They always knew where I was."

"Really, it's no problem. It feels good to have a sister to share with."

Sophie took her choices, along with a bag and went back to her room to finish getting ready. She stopped in the doorway, looked back and smiled at me.

Ryan and Tony drove us to the airport. When we said our goodbyes, Ryan handed me a manila envelope. "Here are some more facts about your possible father. It'll be interesting reading on the plane."

Once we were in the air, I opened the envelope Ryan had given me. Sophie and I put our heads close together and read it at the same time.

Jonathon Gaddu was born in Paris, France on August 9, 1944. His parents were theater performers but never reached stardom. Gaddu attended the International School of Paris and the University of Paris where he earned a Liberal Arts degree. He also spent some time at the Bilingual Acting Workshop.

In 1968 he moved to New York where he studied drama at Julliard. Gaddu had his first off-Broadway success in 1972. He married Roxy Watkins on June 18, 1974. His wife died in 1980. Mr. Gaddu never remarried.

Sophie turned toward me. "If this is true our father wouldn't know about us."

I put my hand on hers. "I don't understand any of this. Why not let us go with him?"

She looked out the window. "We'll have to wait and see."

We didn't talk the rest of the way to the hotel. I was lost in my own thoughts and memories. I guessed my sister was too. Once we settled in we ordered from room service and watched a movie in our room.

We chose to eat our breakfast in the hotel dining room. People watched us as we walked through the lobby and were seated. I glanced around and them staring. They turned away when I looked up. "I guess there aren't many red-headed twins around. Have you seen many plays?"

"A few when Tony and I were in college."

"I wonder if any of them were Gaddu's?"

"I don't know. I didn't pay much attention back then."

After breakfast we stepped outside. The weather was cool with no wind. "Let's walk over to the theater," Sophie suggested.

"I'll put the address in my phone's GPS."

When we arrived we hesitated at the stage door. Sophie laid her hand on my arm. "Are you afraid?"

With my hand on the door, I answered. "I don't think its fear. I wonder what he'll say or do. He's seventy-three. I hope he doesn't have a bad heart."

I took a double take when she said, "Jeez." The word I used all the time.

The hall was eerily quiet. The only light came from a desk near the stage. A man sat tapping his pencil on it as if in deep thought. You couldn't hear our steps on the thickly car-peted aisle. When I spoke to him, he jumped. "Are you Jona-than Gaddu?"

He looked up and the color drained from his wrinkled face. "Why yes, yes I am." He spoke softly, had a low voice, and a thick French accent. He glanced between the two of us several times before he spoke again."I think a better question is, who are you two?"

Sophie answered. "We believe we are the daughters of you and Margaret De Marco."

He pushed his hair back off his face. "It's a lovely thought, but I don't know a Margaret De Marco. My only marriage was to Roxy Watkins. She was wounded in a hit and run accident. She later died at the hospital."

"Was she pregnant?" I asked.

He put his pencil down and crossed his arms. "Yes, the baby was due within a few weeks of her death."

I took a step forward. "We realize this is a shock to you. The two of us didn't know about one another until a few months ago. May we sit down?"

"Yes, of course." A tear rolled down his face. "If you thought you were my daughters, where have you been all of these years?"

Sophie told her story first. "I was raised as the daughter of Dominic De Marco. We have reason to believe Roxy Watkins was Margaret De Marco, his sister. He always let me think he was my father. It was only when I saw my sister's picture in a news article that I became interested in investigating my background."

He stood. "I've heard of him, nothing good, I might add. So, you were raised in New Jersey with a known Mafia leader as your father? What is your name?" He didn't wait for her to answer. He turned to me. "And you?"

"I was raised in St. Charles, Missouri and St. Petersburg, Florida by a woman I found out wasn't my mother. We have not found out who she really is or why they kept us a secret from you or even why they separated us at birth."

He fell into his chair. "And your name is?"

"Kate Nash. It was Kate Madison before I married."

He leaned forward and looked from one of us to the other. "You look exactly like your mother did at your age. It's how I remember her. The thing about dying before your time is that you are forever young in the eyes of your loved ones. It is difficult for me to absorb all of this. Why now?"

I raised, pulled my chair closer to him and spoke to him only when I was situated and could see his eyes. "I'll make this story as short and concise as I can. Later we can fill in the blanks if you want us to. I am a Private Investigator in St. Louis. I had a case that received national attention. Sophie saw it and came to find me. Once we were together, it was impossible to deny we are identical twins."

He motioned for Sophie to bring her chair up to where I was. "My dear wife was in the wrong place at the wrong time. They were never able to find the driver who hit her. She died at the hospital.

"I was in France. I flew home immediately. She was already cremated. They said the only identification she carried didn't give much information. They couldn't find a next of kin. The baby boy died due to the trauma of the accident."

Sophie's face turned red. I didn't know it was anger until she spoke. "You haven't had any interaction with Dominic De Marco? He is and always has been an evil person. He has always had an entire army of thugs to carry out his slightest whim. There are too many coincidences for our story to be false."

I took over. "It can't be a fluke that your wife was cremated before you got to see her body, on March 31^{st,} 1980 and we were born April 1st of the same year.

"Who made such a decision on your behalf? And it seems there was not a baby boy, but twin girls. We have no idea why we were separated or what the reasoning was to keep us a secret. I don't know him as well as Sophie."

He interrupted and answered. "I will never forget the night I found out she was already in a state that made it impossible for me to say goodbye. The doctor's name was Signorelli."

Sophie laid her hand on his. "Our research shows that Roxy Watkins was Margaret De Marco. Margaret died at the hand of a notorious Mafia thug named Mickey Amato in 1988. I know Roxy did not die on our birthday. She came to see me several times a week until I was eight."

Our father slumped back in his chair. "Why would anyone want my beautiful Roxy to die?"

I leaned forward. "We think it was because Margaret was witness to a mob killing. They wanted her to appear dead to protect her. I have a picture of Margaret from her high school yearbook. Is this Roxy?"

He laid his head on the desk. "I don't want to hear any more. It is too much to absorb all at once. I want you to leave now."

Our father was a slight man with a full head of white hair. I knew why I was short. He looked over the glasses that rested on his nose. His cheekbones were high and his movement light as if he was afraid anything he touched would break. He stood, took off his glasses, walked between us. "If there are other details I need to know, I will call you. How did you find Roxy?"

I stood to leave. "She made a movie in late 1979. We stumbled over it a week ago."

"Yes." Sophie stood and moved so she was hip to hip with me. "Did Roxy make a movie?"

"I'm not familiar with it but my Roxy was eccentric and theatrical. I don't doubt she would make a movie I wouldn't know about. I spent a lot of time in France the years we were married. My mother was dying and I stayed months at a time."

Sophie softened her voice. "We were as stunned as you about all of this. We want nothing of you. We hoped if you were our father you would tell us some details about our mother."

He tried to stand but his knees buckled. Sophie grabbed one side and I grabbed the other to steady him until he could stand again. "I need to think about all of this. Don't take me wrong. I believe you are sincere and believe you are telling me the truth. All of it is a shock. When I get it straight in my mind I will call you. Where are you staying?"

At the Dream." We answered in unison.

"Fine, I will reach you there. Will you be in town a few days?"

Sophie answered. "As long as it takes."

CHAPTER 28

We didn't hear from Jonathan Gaddu for three days. During that time I spoke to Ryan who said he was caught up with his work and ready for me to come home.

Tony found out from Missouri Baptist that a woman identified as Roxy Gaddu nee Watkins gave birth to twin girls. The father was listed at Jonathan Gaddu. Mrs. Gaddu was immediately transferred to Honor Hospital where she died later of gunshot wounds. The body was cremated on April 2, 1980.

When Sophie hung up from speaking to Tony she told me what he said. "We know Margaret didn't die at the hospital. We know there were two babies who were given to two different people and that Margaret became Roxy Watkins. What we don't know is why?"

"I have questions too," I said. "What happened to Roxy Watkins when we were eight? It all makes my head spin."

Sophie sat on her bed. "We are closer than we were. We know who our father is and he seems to be unscathed by the Mafia. I wish he would call."

It was as though Sophie wished it into being. The phone rang and when I answered, it was our father. Sophie came as close as she could. I turned the phone toward her so she could eavesdrop.

"Hello."

"Hello, this is Jonathan Gaddu. I wondered if you two ladies would like to join me for dinner at the Fraunces Tavern at eight o'clock tonight."

Sophie shook her head indicating she wanted to go.

"We'll be there. We look forward to seeing you again."

There was a slight pause on his end before he admitted. "I find myself wanting to see the two of you also. Eight o'clock."

He hung up.

It was five thirty so we had plenty of time to get ready. I wasn't familiar with the restaurant so I was lost. "I'm not sure what to wear."

My sister laughed. "I thought I had been almost everywhere in New York, but never to the Faunces. I suggest we look at the menu before we go. I think a simple dress, heels and some nice jewelry."

I Googled it. "I'm a little more vanilla in my food choices. Good thing I looked it up."

She took the phone. "Let me see. I'd go with the House Pate' for an appetizer, roasted corn and spinach ravioli as a main course and a Meyer Lemon Tart for dessert."

She handed the phone back. "Is that what you will get?"

"Most likely, I might be more vanilla than you."

I took a shower and put on a plain blue dress I had bought while we waited for Sophie. She wore a pale green skirt with a cream-colored long sleeve sweater. I threw a shawl over my outfit. She wore my white wool coat.

The taxi dropped us off at exactly eight. The hostess took us to the table like she knew who we were. Our father stood when he saw us.

Dinner was pleasant. He told stories of nights his plays didn't go well. I threw in a couple of antidotes about some of the people Amy and I encountered in our work, and Sophie laughed about how proper the people she lived with were. She added," They were polite as they rid the world of those people who couldn't advance their agenda."

We sat and talked while we had a second glass of wine. Jonathan was the first to speak about our connection. "I indeed believe you are my children. This evening with you two convinced me. Your mannerisms are like watching my beloved Roxy. There are other subtle likenesses I have seen but can't put into words. Take these envelopes. I believe you will treasure what's in them. I must go now. I am an early-to-bed-early-to-rise sort of man. Please call anytime and we'll make plans to meet again."

Sophie and I had made a small packet with our phone numbers, addresses and such. I handed it to him. We all three walked out together. There was a car waiting for him. He kissed us each on both cheeks and said, " Au revoir" as he got into his car.

We stood a moment and watched until he was out of sight. I knew I had tears in my eyes, and I wiped them with the back of my hand. As my twin turned toward me, a tear rolled down her cheek.

We flew home the next day. Since we were so much alike, neither one had much to say. I wanted to review each moment of my first dinner with my father, my real father.

The envelopes he gave us contained photographs of our mother. She looked happy and robust. In one picture, she and her husband stood in front of the Eiffel Tower. I looked at them at least a hundred times and would cherish them forever.

Ryan and Tony were waiting for us at baggage pick up. I was so happy to see him I didn't want to let go. I was excited to tell him about our father and show him the contents of the packet he gave me.

Chili was in the car. She jumped on my lap when I sat down, jumped in the backseat to say hello to Sophie, and back to me where she settled down.

I was so glad to be home. I changed into warm comfy clothes and went to sit in the living room with the other three. Sophie and Tony were deep in conversation. They stopped talking when we entered the room."Is everything okay?" I asked.

Sophie and Tony were on the love seat. She had her feet tucked under her. The same way I liked to sit.

"We were trying to decide when to go to New Jersey. We can't let the house sit and leave the bills unpaid. I also need to get some papers from the safe and open a probate for Dominic's estate."

I turned sideways, put my feet on the couch and leaned back against Ryan. "I thought you didn't think he was dead."

"I don't, but I also know wherever he is, he won't come back. He went to a lot of trouble to fake his death. He killed three people and put them in that car to make sure his death looked real. When I get to the compound and look in the safe, I'll know for sure."

Ryan put one arm around me and joined the conversation. "While you were gone we tried to follow the trail of Roxy Watkins. She made the movie but no one in New York, where it was filmed, ever saw her again. The producer died several years ago, but someone told Neil they didn't even have an address to send her royalties."

Tony took over. "This Roxy Watkins didn't have a social security number, a driver's license, a job record, bank account, or anything else. We think she, with her brother's help, decided she and her daughter were safer if no one knew she was alive. I am convinced she did not know about you, Kate. Ryan hired a skip tracer. A woman of her description lived in a hotel for a few years. She kept to herself."

Sophie moved closer to Tony. "The story is that she witnessed a mob shooting in New York, was identified and killed. There must be more to it."

Ryan got up. "Wine anyone?" Everyone said yes. "My detective said that isn't all she saw. They killed Mickey Amato and his driver as they were walking to court to testify against Martin De Grasse.

"Margaret was a material witness in that case. She overheard De Grasse order and plan the murders of a banker and his family. No one knows how they found out about her or what she heard."

"Yes, Tony said. "The Feds blackmailed her with charges against her family, namely Dominic if she didn't testify. He set up the ruse where she was shot to death and never seen again. We all think you two were collateral damage. First we thought she died in an automobile accident, then a shooting, now a hit and run.

I took a sip of my wine. "I wonder what kind of life a woman with no identity can have."

Ryan handed Sophie a glass of wine. "Like most mothers, her priority was her child. I agree if she did know, she would have never allowed you to be away from her. She went to the Compound every day she could and spent all of her time with Sophie. Tony's mother told us that one day someone came to see Dominic on business and recognized Roxy. She was never seen again. There's no record of her death. We can only go by what Rosa said."

Sophie took a big drink. "I wish I could find Dominic and find out what happened to her. I remember how sweet and gentle she was. As I pull up those memories, I know it was the same women as in the movie. Jonathan verified it was her."

I stood and walked to the kitchen to get another glass of wine. "I know how we could fill in the blanks and find out what happened to Roxy."

"How?" they all asked.

"Mother."

CHAPTER 29

Tony and Sophie cooked dinner for Ryan and me. It was delicious. We had cod stuffed with crab and shrimp, a salad topped with Tony's homemade dressing and chocolate mousse for dessert. As we sat around the table satiated and relaxed, Sophie wanted to talk about what to do next. "I agree we should confront your so-called mother and lean on her to tell us the real truth about what she knows. Tony and I would like to go along on that trip. First, we need to go home and see what and who's there. The longer I stay away, the more complicated it could be to straighten out everything."

Ryan filled his glass with the Moscato that accompanied our meal. "I know you must go. Since you're going back blind, I'd like to send several bodyguards with you."

Sophie slid her glass closer to Ryan for a refill. "I don't think that's necessary. I've known these people for my entire life. No one would hurt me."

Tony looked at her. "I think it's a good idea. The men have been wandering around without supervision for almost two weeks. We don't know if they accepted Martin for Boss, or whether the two leaderless factions have banded together with their own leadership, or they could have disbanded for lack of direction."

I got an unsettled feeling in the pit of my stomach. I hoped Sophie would never go back to that prison. "Would you like Ryan and me to go with you?"

Sophie didn't hesitate. "No. it's not the place for you. If there's someone with a grudge, they won't know if it's you or me. But we do want to go to Florida with you. We'll only be gone a few days."

Ryan took his phone out of his pocket. "When do you want to leave? I'll get the men ready. I'll send six. That should be enough to keep you out of harm's way."

Tony cleared the table. "We would like to leave in the morning. If you don't care, we'll drive. If there's trouble, I know your cars are bulletproof."

No one smiled. "My supervisor, Nathan will take charge of the men. Tell him what you want them to do and where you want them. There'll be an SUV in front of you with three men and one behind you. Keep Kate and me posted. We'll worry."

"I'd like to leave about four am. We won't wake you."

Tony shook hands with Ryan and Sophie hugged me. They went their way to make plans. Ryan and I finished the kitchen chores and took Chili for a long walk. The weather had tuned seasonal. It was below freezing with a cold north wind. The dog didn't seem to care.

My phone rang as we stepped into the elevator for the ride up to the apartment. It was Amy. "Hi partner. Are you ready to spend some time at the office? It's a mess. We have callbacks, bills to pay and business to discuss."

I took my scarf and hat off as we talked. "Yes. It would be a pleasant break and I'll fill you in on my father. Want to meet at the office?"

She laughed. "How about Starbucks in U City? We haven't talked in a long while."

"Okay, I'll be there."

Ryan stood behind me when I turned around. "Am I going to lose you to a case before we have any time to spend on the house which is sitting empty and forlorn waiting for a family?"

I couldn't help but give big him a giant hug. "We'll have the rest of the evening and until noon tomorrow. We need to tend to our office and some book work."

He let me go. "It's too late to shop tonight. Let's go over and look at the house. You couldn't possibly remember much about it."

I put my coat on again. "Okay let's go."

The house was more beautiful than I had remembered. The rooms were spacious. I couldn't see the light pattern because the sun had set. I imagined the light came in from every direction. We made a sketch of the rooms and the window and door placement so we could get furniture to fit each room.

Ryan beamed from ear to ear. I was no longer nervous. We had shared the same space long enough for me to know it was wonderful. "Is there anything from the apartment you would like to bring over here?"

I mentally walked through the Penthouse. "No, only my personal belongings, I love the thought of decorating the house with you. Is there anything from the Mansion you want?"

"Actually, there is my desk. It was my father's and his father's before that."

I took his hand. "Where do you want to put it?"

"I thought we could make an office out of the den. We have more rooms here than we will use. It's large enough for both of us to have a part of it and still have a love seat and a couple of chairs."

He faced me. "I think it'll be perfect here. The only thing that would be better would be if you would marry me." In his other hand he held a tiny box.

It was the last thing I expected at that time. I stood stunned while he opened the plush red container and took out a ring. I had never seen anything like it. When I hesitated he told me, "It was my mother's engagement ring. I won't push you into marriage. Since in my heart, I know you love me and we're heading toward getting married, I would like you to have this."

Ryan slipped the ruby and diamond ring on my finger. It was hard to look away from it. "I do love you. I have for a long time."

He pulled me into a hug and kissed me. "If I had known all it took to have you say you loved me was a ring, I would have given it to you sooner."

He kissed me again.

CHAPTER 30

When we got back to the Penthouse, Ryan and I toasted our engagement. We had a lovely night and lingered in bed until after ten the next morning. I sat up and put my feet on the floor. "I hate the thought of leaving this warm bed but I need to get ready, I'm supposed to meet Amy at noon."

"I need to go home and do some work. I'm so glad our belongings will all be in the same place."

I smiled at him and headed for the shower. I couldn't decide whether to take my ring off or leave it on while I showered. I had my hand up so I could admire it. Ryan came in. "I thought I'd join you."

"I'm trying to decide if I should leave it on or take it off while I shower."

He pulled me to him. "Wear it. If anything happens to it, we can fix it."

I leaned back so I could see his face. "But it was your mothers."

"I know, rings can be replaced, you can't. Enjoy it."

I kissed him and stepped into the shower that had been running the entire time. The hot water felt good. Ryan washed my back. "I can't play," I said. "I want to be warm and dry before I go out in the cold."

He let go of me. "Spoil-sport."

I put on slacks and a heavy sweater, a ski jacket, a scarf and a hat. Ryan said I reminded him of *Nanook of the North.*

Amy sat at a table with two lattes, bagels and cream cheese. She was dressed almost the same as I. We both chose black.

I joined her. "We can't stay here long, I'll melt."

She looked me up and down. "I know. I couldn't decide if I should get drinks or not. It'll take a half an hour to get my clothes off if I need to go to the bathroom."

I shed my hat, scarf, gloves, and coat. "So what's our plan?"

She pushed my latte in front of me and picked her own up to take a drink. I grinned and stuck my hand out so she couldn't miss my ring. "Ryan gave it to me last night. We went to look at the house. I turned around and there he was, ring in hand."

"Congratulations. Did you two set a date?"

"Heavens no, I'm not ready to get married again."

Amy put her hand on my arm. "Don't wait too long. You deserve to be happy, and I don't think I know another couple as compatible as you and Ryan."

I couldn't help but ask her about Nathan and Jake. "Have you heard from Jake?"

"No, we decided a clean break is best. I realized I miss the long newsy phone calls we shared more than the time we spent together. I hate to admit it, but had he not found some-one else I might have had that relationship forever. It was comfortable."

I drank my coffee and ate the bagel. "How are things with Nathan?"

She lit up, her eyes sparkled and she giggled a little. "We went to the wedding. I haven't had that good of an evening in years. He's been doing your work at the agency. I tried to pay him but he said it was an assignment from Ryan. I think he must wake up in a good mood and go to bed in one."

"So do you know personally if he wakes up happy or not?"

Her face turned crimson red. "No, he hasn't even kissed me goodnight. I hope he doesn't look at us as a platonic pair. I would like it to progress."

"You heard Ryan. Nathan's interested. Maybe you should give him a nudge."

She laughed.

The office was toasty warm. I took off my coat. "Can we afford to have the heat on like this?"

Amy handed me the checkbook that lay on her desk. "Maybe you should take a look."

I went into my own office and sat down. "How did we get so far ahead?"

She sat in the chair across from me. "It happens when your partner is famous. Since Sophie gained the spotlight as you, the phone has been ringing off the phone. Many of them have been skip tracing. Nathan and I had access to Ryan's equipment. We could sometimes finish four a day."

"Wow. How many do you have pending?" I asked.

She walked back to her office and returned with a manila folder almost an inch thick. "These are only the ones we have to leave the office to investigate. There's another one in there from Southern Marshall Foundries. They want a background check on all of their employees. They're talking about offering stock to their workers and switch to employee-owned. I don't follow their reasoning, but they are paying big bucks for us to do it. Again, with Ryan's machines, they are each back within a few hours."

"It looks as though you don't need me."

"Oh yes I do. I love to work with Nathan, but I have to dress up all the time, full makeup, you get the idea."

"Amy, you like him more than you want to admit."

She smiled but ignored my comment. "This one's interesting. Someone was stealing out of cars in the Central Neighborhood of St. Peters. It's been going on for several weeks. Now they steal packages off of porches."

"They can't catch them on camera?" I asked.

"No. He wears a ski mask and there doesn't seem to be a getaway car nearby. It's contained in a fifteen block area. Here's a drawing of the area. Makes me think it's someone in the neighborhood."

I took the map from her. "It does. It would explain why whoever's stealing is close enough to walk home. What do the police say?"

"They always come after the deed's done. They patrol but can't be everywhere at the same time. If the culprit knows the neighborhood well enough, he could take shortcuts through yards and never get caught. I'm ready to tackle it."

I was excited about doing what I was trained to do. For the next ten minutes I told her about Jonathon Gaddu, and Tony, and Sophie going back to New Jersey to see what the status was there. "When the two of them return, the four of us are going to pay one more visit to Mother and try to get her to tell the truth since half the cat is out of the bag already."

She sat straighter in her chair. "I don't care how long you're gone. I want you to get your life back. I can't imagine finding out your entire childhood was built on lies."

"Before we leave today, I'm going to make a copy of your map. Maybe I can find a pattern."

She went to the copy machine and made two copies and handed me one. "Okay, see you tomorrow. Let's meet here and take my truck."

When I arrived back at the apartment Ryan was watching PBS. It was the Life and Times of Billy the Kid. He looked up when I stood behind him. "Since when are you interested in Billy the Kid?"

He didn't look away from the TV. "Since Chili fell asleep on me and I didn't want to bother her."

I plopped down beside him with such force Chili bounced and woke up. She stretched, yawned, climbed over on me and went immediately back to sleep. "There, you're free."

"You just burst my bubble. I was sure she couldn't do without me."

"I moved closer to him. "Can I mend your feelings with a kiss?"

He pushed the button on the remote that turned the television off. "No, but two or three might help. He picked up the map I had laid on the table. "What's this? Are you and Amy searching for buried treasure?"

I told him about the neighborhood thefts. "The police gave Amy a map of the area. It has the houses marked, the day, the time they were robbed and what was taken. We each took a copy to see if we could pick out a pattern."

"Can I help? I love a good map."

We moved to the table in front of the balcony window, pulled our chairs closer together, and studied the map.

We drew lines from the first robbery scene to the second, to the third and so on. When we were finished, I traced the route with my finger. "It's so random, it has a pattern. Do you see it?"

He looked at the map again and to me. "Have you ever heard of the Gambler's Paradox?"

"Yes, I've heard of it, but it's all about square roots and expectations. I think whoever the thief goes about it in a methodical way. Look." I took the pencil and put the point on the paper. Follow the map with me: the first block, fifth house, tenth block, sixth house and so on. According to that pattern, he will be in the third block, tenth house Tuesday. That address in 2527 S. Windsor. Do you agree?"

Before he could answer, my phone rang. It was Amy, she seemed excited. "I figured it out. It's a pattern."

I interrupted her. "Where will he be tomorrow?"

"Nowhere, but Tuesday he'll be at 2527…"

I finished her sentence for her. "South Windsor."

"Great minds," she said. "Tomorrow's only Monday. I guess we get a day off."

"Okay, see you." I hung up told Ryan I had the next day off.

He took my hand and we went back to the couch. "Good. Tomorrow we can go to the house and pick the paint colors for the rooms. I don't know about you, but I think the rooms don't match our personalities."

I sat. "Me too, let's go to the paint store and get some swatches of the colors we like. We can get one for the painter and one to take with us to pick out the furnishings. I'd like to take Chili. She has been alone too much lately."

The next morning after breakfast we headed to our new house. Ryan had Chili under his arm. She was content and didn't want to come to me when we got into the truck.

At the house, we let Chili out in the backyard. She was in heaven. She ran and played. I didn't realize she could run as fast as she could. Ryan and I strolled through the house deciding on colors. The rest of the day we shopped.

The next day I was at the office at nine o'clock sharp. We drove two blocks south of where we predicted the thief would strike next.

As we pulled up to the curb Amy looked at me. "Now that we're here, I see a problem."

"I see it too. There are six blocks of houses behind us with sixteen homes on a block."

Amy looked around at our location. "I don't know why we didn't think of this. We don't know which way he's coming from or which way he'll try to escape."

I rolled down my window. "If we don't figure something out soon, we'll blow our opportunity to catch him."

She put her gloves and hat on. "I'll duck behind the bushes of the house next door. The only other place to hide is in that playhouse in the side yard of that house over there."

I bundled up and ran to my spot. When I was settled I looked to see if Amy was well hidden. She was. I knew where she was and I couldn't see her. The time dragged. With the cold closing in on me and the lack of movement I got sleepy. My eyes were about to close again when I saw movement.

I perked up immediately. It was a person weaving between the houses, stopping now and then to look around. There wasn't a package on the porch of the house we had picked out. There was one at the house where Amy hid and one in a box the owners had constructed to keep their deliveries dry at the house two doors away from where I was.

My gun was in my inside coat pocket where I could easily reach it. It was fifteen minutes before he reached his target. He looked around and walked backward to avoid the camera installed on the corner that could identify him. He opened the lid on the box and took out the package it contained.

He weaved back the direction he came but by a different route. When he was out of my field of vision I ran to the truck. Amy sprinted to the passenger's side and jumped in. "Go. Go."

When I got to the next street I turned left and drove slowly down it looking in every nook and cranny. Amy got a glimpse of him two houses up on the other side of the street. I sped up and stopped one lot behind him. Amy jumped out of the truck and ran around the other side of the yard so she'd be in front of him.

The robber ran. Amy stuck her foot out before he had a chance to get too far away from her. When he went down, he grabbed Amy's leg and took her down with him. As I left the truck it was still rolling. The man was on top of her and about to hit her when I stuck my Glock in his nose. "Move and I'll shoot you."

He was a big man. In one push he rolled Amy off of him and into my wrist. My gun fell out of my hand but I didn't stop. When he was nearly out of our reach, he looked back at me and said. "Little lady, you need a different occupation."

He made a mistake. He stopped to catch his breath. He paused long enough for Amy to grab his leg. He didn't fall, but it slowed him down enough for me to catch up. His back was to me. I pulled my leg back as far as I could and kicked him between the legs. He fell like a bag of rocks and writhed in pain. I reached up and pulled the ski mask off his head. It was the subdivision president who hired us. While Amy called 911, I nudged his hands—they were still holding his crotch—with my foot and told him, "Don't ever call me little lady."

The police were there within minutes. Amy and I spent the time wiping the dirt and mud off of our clothes.

She walked closer to me so the perp couldn't hear her. "You're getting pretty good at dropping men with a kick."

I didn't care if he heard or not. "No one should call me *little lady*. Because a woman is short doesn't mean she is inept."

An officer came to interview us. "Do you have some identification?" He spoke to both of us. We each showed him our PI badges and licenses. He handed us one of his cards and told us to drop by the station to read and sign our statements sometime the next day.

Amy dropped me by the office to pick up my car. "No need to come to the office tomorrow. I will need a day to get warm and tend to my bruises."

I couldn't help but agree. 'I'll call you late morning."

I rode home with my heater on high. I was still cold when I got there.

CHAPTER 31

No one greeted me when I stepped off the elevator. Ryan's truck was parked in the lot and even if he was busy, Chili never missed an opportunity to welcome me home.

I scanned the room. A light shone from the hallway that led to the master bedroom. The light got brighter as I got closer. There on the bed lay Ryan, fully dressed, propped up on two pillows with a novel on his chest and one hand on Chili, who was sound asleep on her back with all four feet in the air.

I'm not a quiet person, but I didn't have the heart to wake them. There were some PJ's hanging in the bathroom. With one hand I got them and with the other hand, I took a quilt off the shelf.

They were so cute and comfortable. I stood in the hallway and watched them for a long while, went to the living room, changed into my comfy clothes and fell asleep on the couch.

My phone rang. It was on the other side of the room. I scrambled to get it before it woke my roommates. "Hi, how's it going up there?"

"We're about done. We should be back by Wednesday evening. It was as I told you. I own everything expect for the money he took from the safe and another fortune in bearer bonds I forgot about. He has enough money to lavishly support ten people. He left notes in the safe about how much money he wanted me to give everyone. Your name was on the list. There is a post-it note stuck to it that says, and I quote. *It's a good thing you didn't want to be an actress. You're horrible at it.*"

I was flabbergasted. "So he knew it was me all along. It makes me more anxious to confront Denise Madison or whoever my mother is. There are some pictures of his boys and wife that aren't here."

I looked up. Ryan stood at the door with Chili in his arms. "What about the business and his men?"

"He let them all go with more than generous severance. If they like the Mafia life, we heard Jimmy Angelo has announced the territory as his and he is daring anyone to dispute it."

I motioned for Ryan to come sit beside me. "Sounds like you've been busy. Safe travels and we'll see you soon."

Chili crawled out of Ryan's arms and came to me. I finally got the kisses I expected hours ago. "How long were you there? Did you hear any of that?"

"Most of it, want to fill me in?"

"Sure." For the next few minutes I repeated the conversation for him.

I rubbed his arm. "It is barely ten o'clock, why are you so tired?"

He moved closer. "Once in awhile, it all catches up and I need to sleep. Tonight is one of those nights."

"Are you sure that is all it is?"

He kissed me on the cheek. "Yes. Let's turn in."

We must have both been tired. We slept all through the night and until mid-morning when Chili insisted she had to go outside.

CHAPTER 32

Sophia and Tony looked exhausted when they arrived at the apartment.

Tony took their luggage to the bedroom. "Ryan, I hate to ask, but can you help me carry some of our belongings from the car?"

Before Ryan had a chance to respond, the buzzer signaled someone wanted to come upstairs. He walked over and said back over his shoulder. "I don't think either one of us needs to make another trip. Nathan and the men have all of it in the lift and are on their way up."

Sophie hugged me and Ryan and petted Chili as she begged for attention. "I have so much to tell you two."

I rescued her from Chili's constant flitting. "Sorry, you know everyone is a new person for the first five minutes."

She reached over to take Chili back. "Actually, I missed her. Waking up without the help of a cold nose on your cheek is overrated. Once Tony and I are settled, we plan to get a dog. Pets are something we weren't allowed to have when we were children."

Ryan and Tony moved the boxes and bags into the room they stayed in. I heard Ryan tell Tony, "Let's put this stuff in the next bedroom. No one uses it. It'll give you much more room."

Tony walked down the hall to look at the other bedroom. "Are you sure?"

"I'm sure. Kate and I are moving to our house as soon as the rooms are painted and the furniture arrives."

"Great. Sophie and I are sure we don't want to live in the East where her name is associated with the mob."

Sophie joined them. I heard the conversation because they stood in the hallway. "He's right. When I go into law practice I want to use my own name. I will be Mrs. Anthony Marino, except for my job."

Ryan glanced my way. "It's a subject we haven't approached yet. Kate and Amy have a following under Nash and Perkins. I've got mixed feelings. There's never been a Mrs. Ryan Meade and I like the thought of it being Kate. Half of me wonders why a woman is supposed to lose part of her identity and change her last name."

I walked over and gave him a kiss. "I didn't think we discussed marriage yet."

He didn't back down. "We both know it'll come with time. I could never leave Chili."

I playfully poked him in the ribs. "How long has it been since the two of you have eaten?"

Tony rubbed his belly as if he were starving. "Nathan got us some burgers when we filled up the car the last time. It wasn't exactly a meal. I'm too tired to cook and I don't want any more fast food."

Ryan patted him on the back. "I can fix this problem." He looked at his watch. "Can you wait an hour?"

Sophie put her arm around his waist. "Yes, he can wait. He isn't going to faint or anything."

An hour later, the elevator called us. Ryan went down and came back with four large boxes. He barely sat them on the table before he was summoned again. This trip he carried two large boxes and a loaf of Italian bread. It happened again. "This is the last time, I promise. Kate will you get some plates and Tony would you open a bottle of wine?"

"Red or white?"

Ryan came over to the table and opened the boxes and removed real glass containers of food. "There's a large choice, so let's have one of each."

The boxes contained a Chinese dinner including Crab Rangoon and Egg Drop Soup. There was Rigatoni with Sand dabs, Caesar Salad, and warm bread. Last but not least was Shrimp, crab cakes, salmon with lemon sauce, baked potatoes and four huge brownies.

Sophie sat and looked at all the food. "This is more than generous, Ryan."

"My pleasure," he answered. My chef from The Magnolia was happy to do it. Let's toast to good food, family, love, and friendship."

We didn't talk about ourselves or our problems during dinner. I was relaxed and happy.

Together we cleaned up the mess and retired to the living room with our glasses and our bellies full. It was time to talk about Dominic and the lessons learned while they were gone.

Sophie related the facts of their trip. "I told you some of this on the phone the other night. I'll try not to repeat myself. I know from what I found in the house, the accounts and from talking to the men. Dominic had this all planned."

Tony took a sip of his wine. "The supposed marriage between Johnny and Sophie was a ruse to get the Lombardi family to let their guard down. His fatal mistake was trusting Dominic. As soon as they had Johnny in a situation where he relaxed around them, he was assassinated. The murder of Samuel was a cover-up so they would all be too busy to look for Johnny until the De Marco family was out of harm's way."

Sophie reached into a packet she had next to her on the floor. "This is a sample of Dominic's sense of humor. "

I opened the letter. *Dear Kate,*

It's a good thing you didn't try to make it in acting. Sorry you are so distraught about your childhood. Here is a little something to ease the disappointment.

Sophie reached for the packet again and handed me a cashier's check. "This has got to be a joke or a hoax. Why would he give me this?"

Ryan came over and looked over my shoulder. "I guess you won't have to worry about whether the bills will get paid or not."

Sophie tried to put an explanation with the check. "I know you're shocked that Dominic would leave you a check for one million dollars. I went to the bank where it was print-ed. It is indeed real and yours."

I read the letter again. "He knows Denise Madison, my mother. He has to. How else would he know about my false childhood? As soon as you are rested, it is time to call on her. She knows more and doesn't want us to know."

Sophie, Tony, and Ryan all said "yes" at the same time.

I took another look at the amount of the check. "I don't want his money."

Sophie moved over to sit beside me."Yes, you do. You deserve it. Give it away. There has to be something you are passionate about. You're not the only one who received a letter and a check. Tony received one as did his mother and the principles of the now-defunct crime mob he represented."

Tony filled my glass with more wine and offered more to the others. "I had the same reaction as you. My letter said he didn't want me to marry someone who held the purse strings so I should have some money of my own. As far as we could tell from the checkbook, he gave everyone between fifty-thousand and a million depending on their standing and loyalty to the family. One of the biggest checks went to my mother, and one went to your mother."

I looked at Ryan for guidance. "That answers a multi-tude of questions. Now that we know who, the only question left is why. As for the money, I agree with Sophie. Give it to charity."

I was weary and didn't want to talk about Dominic's money. He made me and my sister's lives lies, and to ease his conscience he wanted to throw money at it. "Let's go to Mother's."

Sophie stood. "Yes, as soon as we get a good night's sleep. Maybe you should make a stop at a bank. Ryan can show you how to arrange the accounts so they're all insured. We're going to rest now. Any time after noon tomorrow is good to go to Florida."

We all said our goodnights. Ryan and I took a long walk with the dog. I didn't have anything to say. I wondered if I should tell Amy and maybe give her some of the money.

I tossed and turned so much I woke Ryan several times. Once I must have dozed off because Ryan shook me gently to tell me he had a hot bath waiting for me. He thought it would calm me down. As he left the bathroom he stopped. "The money need not make you anxious. As close as you and Amy are, I would think long and hard before I told her the details of your new found wealth. Money has a way of driving a wedge into any relationship. Now soak and relax. Everything will work out."

Ryan again was wise. By the time the bath water cooled. I was drowsy. Once I slipped under the warm covers, I slept like a baby.

A noise scared me. The room was dark so I knew it was the middle of the night. What woke me was a dream or a nightmare. I wasn't sure which. Denise Madison was at my high school graduation. I asked about my childhood and she handed me a check for a million dollars. At my college graduation, I said I wished my father was alive to see me get my degree. She gave me a check. The dream went through every highpoint in my life. At every occasion she handed me money.

The check was on the dining room table. I got up, walked in and looked at it for a long time. I tore it into a dozen small pieces, put it in a small bowl, took it out on the balcony and burned it. I let the ashes drift away in the morning breeze.

I crawled back into bed, snuggled up to Ryan, and went to back to sleep.

The alarm went off at eight. "Why do we need an alarm?" I asked.

"We have a lot to do today. It'll take awhile to straighten out your money and put it someplace safe. I chartered a plane to fly us all to Florida. We need to be at the airport by about two."

I wondered how he would take the news that I was a millionaire for less than twelve hours.

He walked around the bed and sat down next to me "Is there something wrong? Do you still want to visit your mother?"

I laid my hand on his leg. "It's not that. I tore up Dominic's bribery check up and burned it. No one should be able to negate your life and give you money thinking it would ease the wrong that was done. The money will go into Sophie's account and she can give it away."

"I would have been surprised if you kept the money." I hugged him. "So now we have some extra time we didn't think we would have, right?"

"Right."

We made good use of our free time.

CHAPTER 33

The four of us arrived in St. Petersburg in time to check into a motel, have a great dinner, and discuss our plan for the next day—and Mother.

Sophie sat with her feet tucked under her on the couch next to Tony. "I think we should all go and not give her any warning."

He put his arm on the back of the couch where she sat. "I have learned you can find out more if no one knows you're coming."

I sat at the desk. "I agree. Let's go early afternoon so if she's teaching, she'll be done for the day, and home."

Ryan got out of the chair he sat in. "It's late. Since we all could use the rest, I propose we meet in the lobby at eleven. We'll have brunch somewhere and head out there."

We all agreed. They went next door to their own room.

The weather was warm and sunny. A gentle breeze blew in from the ocean. Ryan and I went for a walk on the beach.

Tony rented a car. The ride to Mother's was quiet which made it longer than ever. He parked a block from the house.

We walked the rest of the way. I thought it best to go to the back and go in through the door off the deck.

When Ryan opened the door, we walked through the empty kitchen and into the den. Mother sat in her favorite chair and appeared to be interested in a magazine. A man lounged on the couch, his face covered with a ball hat and his head rested on a pillow.

He sat up; the hat fell to the cushion. And there sat Dominic De Marco. Mother looked up and dropped the magazine to her lap. It dawned on me, she had never seen Sophia and me together before. "Why are you here?" She said it the way you'd talk to an intruder.

I looked at Dominic. "I believe a better question is what's *he* doing here? He's dead, you know."

Her face paled. "We can explain all of this."

I couldn't keep the contempt out of my voice. "Hopefully you can explain it better than you did last time I was here."

Sophie walked to Dominic and stood in front of him. "You look pretty good for a dead man."

His hair was long. I'd say he hadn't had a haircut since he left the Compound. He was dressed in well-worn jeans and a polo style shirt with no visible logo. "What three people had to die in that car for you to get the luxury of sitting in a condo by the beach?"

He looked up at her. "They were homeless. No one will miss them." He sounded surly and unrepentant. "My, you two have a lot of anger for two women who grew up with every advantage, including college and law school."

I looked from Mom to Dominic. "Do you think that's enough to make up for kidnapping two babies, lying about our heritage and making our entire lives a lie?"

Ryan came to me and wrapped his arms around me from behind. "This will not get us anywhere. We'll all sit down and listen to the story I am sure these two would like to share now that it makes no difference to anyone but these two women."

Since *neither Mother* nor Dominic offered us a seat, we sat where we wanted. Tony sat next to Dominic, Ryan and I sat side by side on a loveseat, and Sophie sat on the other side of the room where she could see everyone clearly.

Dominic ran his hand through his hair. "We don't owe you an explanation." He looked Sophie in the eye. "Since you're my only daughter, I will explain."

I leaned forward and looked at the woman. "Who are you?

Denise looked at Dominic. It looked as though she wanted his okay to answer. "I'm Denise Madison."

I couldn't believe her answer. "One question, one lie."

Tony crossed his arms over his chest. "Let me tell you what we know, and you can correct our facts or fill in the blanks. We know Denise Madison died in a car crash in 1970. Her driver's license, social security card, and credit cards were not used until 1975 when she miraculously came back to life as a college graduate and taught high school. It happens to follow the same timeline as Louise De Marco's death.

We stared at her. The blood seemed to drain from her face. She slumped in her chair.

Dominic spoke up. "I'm your uncle. Your mother was my sister?"

Sophie asked. "If our mother was a De Marco, who's Roxy Watkins?"

Dominic grinned. "It was a name she used to hide her identity from people she didn't want to find her."

"What people? Her husband thought her name was Roxy Watkins."

He turned toward me. "The ones that eventually killed her. Did you meet Jonathon? I've never even met him. I considered him a diversion to keep my sister busy while she was in exile."

Ryan joined the conversation for the first time. "Wouldn't it be easier to tell us the story instead of playing twenty questions and making derogatory statements about their mother and father?"

Denise chimed in. "We would like to have a life after today. You know more than you should now. "

I leaned forward and glared at her. "We also know you were never a surgical nurse, there was not a Dr. Signorelli, and Sally Jeffers was a janitor and not a nurse."

Sophie chimed in. "Our mother was not a Lombardo, she was not killed in a shootout in 1980, but she was shot to death in 1988. We were not born at Honor Hospital but at Missouri Baptist to Roxy Watkins and Jonathon Gaddu." Sophie stretched her legs out in front of her. "We want you to fill in the gaps in our story. You can start by telling us why our birth certification has an alias listed as our mother's name."

Dominic put the ball cap back on his head. "We've kept the secrets this long, why not let it go? You will put us in danger."

Tony tapped his fingertips on the arm of the couch. I knew it to be a sign he was irritated. "How can you be in danger? The De Marco crime syndicate is defunct as is the Lombardi family."

Denise glared at her. "If you believe those two families are the only danger from the Mafia, you are naïve."

I asked again. "Who are you?"

"I'm Louisa De Marco, just like you figured out. I'm your aunt. Margaret was our youngest sister."

"Sophie kicked her shoes off and tucked her legs under her. "So our father is Jonathon Gaddu, the play write, and our mother was Margaret De Marco. That part is true."

Dominic looked at Sophie. "Yes, how did you figure that out?"

It was Sophie's chance to grin. "My sister is a private investigator. We'll ask the questions and you answer them. Why didn't you give us to our father?"

"Your father is a soft man who couldn't stand up for ten minutes to the people we were protecting your mother from.

He had no idea she had ties to the Mafia. I would have had to come out and burst his bubble about his beautiful red-haired wife. She was safe until you were six. Jonathon was in France with his dying mother. A movie was being shot around New York. She had always wanted to be in the movies. I can't remember a time when she put anyone else's safety ahead of her own desires."

Ryan asked. "Why don't we cut to the chase? What did their mother do, see, or hear that put her in such mortal danger? And what happened to her? Also, while we're at it," he glanced at Denise, "Why did you split these women up when they were babies?"

Dominic stood. "If we are going to tell you all of that, I need a drink. Anyone else?"

Denise stood also. "I'll go and help."

Tony put his hand up. "You rest. I'll go with him. I'd feel much better if the two of you were not alone together. He moved his arm in a sweeping manner to include, Sophie, Ryan, and me. "All of us are weary of this entire mystery. These women deserve to know the answers to all the questions Ryan asked."

Dominic didn't say a word. He left the room with Tony at his heels. A few minutes later, they were back with iced tea and condiments. Once we were all settled, Dominic opened up, "Your mother, Margaret De Marco was vacationing with her sister Louise in Las Vegas." He pointed to Kate's mother. "Margie wanted to shop and Louise didn't. She took off on her own and left the strip to find a candy shop she'd heard about. Little did she know that the Vegas Mob used the back of that location as a meeting place. There was no *closed sign* on the door and the inside wasn't dark. Your mother went in. She wandered around looking at things when she heard gunfire. Three men ran out of the back room, through the shop, and out the door. She ran at the first shot, but they were moving so fast, one of them knocked her down so hard it broke her leg.

"The men left in a car. There were no cell phones then. She stayed on the concrete until someone who heard the shots called 911. Margie ended up in the hospital with her sister at her side. You were there Louise, tell them what happened."

"It was cold. She was in shock, badly bruised and suffered a compound fracture. They kept her overnight for observation. In the wee hours of the morning, two men came into the room. One man covered Margie's mouth and nose so she couldn't get a breath. He told us he didn't know who she was, but he would find out. If she ever told a soul, they would kill her. He looked up and read her information. Margaret Dc Marco. The other man put a gun to my head and warned me too. I was sure Margie would be dead by the time the man removed his hand. At first, she flailed her arms and kicked her feet. By the time he let go she was still."

Sophie didn't seem to think it was a good explanation for what happened to us. "How did that warrant what you two did to us?"

Dominic leaned forward and rested his forearms on his knees. "You have always been impatient Sophia. If we don't tell you what led up to our decision, you will never understand. Kate, are you as impatient as your sister?"

When I didn't answer he continued, "When my sisters came home from Vegas, they were terrified. I found a dead girl's identity for Louise, and Margaret chose Roxy Watkins. She was a flamboyant and reckless young woman. There were thousands of Watkins in the world, Roxanne was common."

Louise interrupted. "Our sister was always enamored with the arts. Roxy came from Roxie Hart in the play Chicago. She knew every Broadway play. That's how she met Jonathon Gaddu. Once the Ricoh Crime family found out she was one of us, and what we did, it was all out war. We faked my death. My sister would not do that, she changed her name and made a permanent move to New York, where she met and married Gaddu. She kept him in the dark about who she actually was.

The movie came out. The Ricoh family found out who she was and came after her. She was pregnant but didn't know it was twins. Once when she was alone in St. Louis she was gunned down on Laclede's Landing. She was shot five times. They took her to Missouri Baptist Hospital where she had twins. You were almost two months old when she was well enough to leave the hospital.

"To save her and you, we only told her about one baby. We planted in the news that she didn't survive her wounds."

I was livid. "Who decided who became a De Marco and who stayed with my *so-called mother?*"

He glared at me but answered. He pointed to Sophie. "She was hardy. It was iffy as to whether you would live. Louise always wanted a baby and was willing to make the sacrifice to put in the time it would take to get you well—if you did get well."

"So in essence, you threw one away and kept the other? I guess you believe *in survival of the fittest.*" Ryan put his hand on my knee, and I stopped talking.

Ryan shook his head. "This is unbelievable."

My sister looked at me. "It's believable from a man who kills people, sells drugs to children, and puts three men in a car and sends them to their death so he can escape."

Dominic leaned back and looked relaxed. I doubt anyone had talked to him like that for years. "Let's not get hostile. I 'm not required to tell you anything."

"No, you aren't. Your hospitality is humbling," Sophie said.

Dominic got up. "I'm done with this for now. I need something to eat. Anyone want to join me?"

He and Louise went into the kitchen. Ryan and Tony followed.

Tony turned back toward me. "The De Marco's always like to stay in control, even if they're sinking in quicksand."

When the four of them came back into the room, Louise and Dominic's attitudes had changed. Neither of them spoke a word. Ryan stood directly in front of Dominic. "I don't know what you think is going on here, but you had best finish your story."

Dominic stood nose to nose with Ryan. "You can't talk to me like that. I'm a powerful man and you don't want to anger me. I can ruin you."

Tony stood next to Ryan. "Sorry big man, but you're no longer on top. What you are is a kidnapper, murderer, and drug dealer who would get five or six life sentences in Joliet."

"Tony, you and your lover would be in the next cells. Everyone knows you're a *made man* in one of the nation's largest Mafia families. And you, my dear niece, have been involved your entire life."

Sophie walked over and stood between the men. "I'll take my chances. I have a signed affidavit that Daniel Lombardi was murdered by Johnny Danko, not Tony. We all know it's down in the books as the killing that allowed him to take the Omerta."

The Mafia boss clinched his fits. Ryan pushed him back into his seat. Everyone turned around when I addressed Louise. "You're no better, kidnapping and pretending to be a mother."

She plopped down.

Everyone returned to their original seats. I tried to get the conversation started again. "Listen, we don't want to be here any more than you to do. Fact is, no one is going anywhere until I'm satisfied I know the story of my life. Dominic, you can move on to where you were going before we found you. And *mother* you can go back go teaching, your bridge club and telling the lies about the achievements of your only daughter."

Ryan stopped me again. "Let's pick up where we left off."

Dominic let out an audible huff. "Your mother was afraid to be away from the Compound. She came every day until you were about eight, Sophie. I'm surprised you don't remember."

"I remember. But I don't ever remember a time when she was there in the evening."

"We put her in a guest house four miles from the Compound. She had more guards than the President. One day she decided to go for a walk. It was foggy, two men went with her, but they lost her. She was found three days later floating in the river. She had been shot in the head. So first we buried Margie and then Roxy. That's about it."

"Who was cremated when our mother was supposed to have died the first time?"

Louise answered in a broken voice as if she were crying. "No one, that's why we had her transferred to Honor."

Sophie paced. I smiled because that's how I did my best thinking. "Did it ever dawn on you in all of those years to tell us about one another? Once our mother was dead, what possible difference could it have made?" She looked at Louise. "And if you loved Kate so much, and she was not involved in crime, why didn't you tell her?"

Louise answered first. "I lived the lie so long, I believed it myself." She leaned forward so she could see me. "I gave you every advantage."

I tried not to let the emotion that had welled up in me come out in my voice. "Except the right to my heritage and the decision to decide for myself what I wanted to do with the truth about who I am."

Dominic addressed Sophie. "You had everything, and when I left, I made you nearly a billionaire." He also looked at me. "I left you a millionaire. I can't be all bad."

My sister had a lightness in her voice. "I have set up a foundation. All your money will go to the homeless, drug rehab and hungry children. I kept only what I earned and was in my personal savings. Thinking you were dead, I turned all my journals over to the FBI. I hope it stops all the other criminals you associated with."

"And I tore up my check. You can't put a dollar amount on what you did to us."

Dominic was done. He stood and no one tried to stop him. "You are foolish women. We have told you the story of your lives. Now get out. I hope never to see either one of you again."

We left. No one offered a goodbye. No one turned around. I heard the door close and lock behind us.

CHAPTER 34

We went back to the motel. Ryan notified the pilot we would fly out the next morning. We had a great dinner and planned to retire early.

"Kate. Want to walk on the beach with me?"

I grinned. "Sure sis. Guys, we won't be long."

Sophie took my hand. We walked to the beach and sat in the sand. "Now that we're alone, I want to know your feelings about what we've learned in the last few months."

I had to take a moment. "I feel hurt and betrayed. On the other hand, I have you."

"I feel blessed to have found you also. But I mean how do you really feel about Dominic and Louise?"

"I think they are the scum of the earth. They lied for almost thirty-five years without taking anything into consideration but their own goals."

She turned toward me and took a piece of paper from her pocket. "I made a list of all the lies. He claimed to be my father. She claimed to be your mother. They lied about the circumstances of our birth. They kidnapped two children. Dominic has no redeeming qualities."

"I know. Mother let me think all our money came from her job at Honor. In reality it came from organized crime. She fabricated a father and made up elaborate stories about him and his parents. She even went into great detail about the difficulty of her labor when I was born."

Sophie shook her head. "What do you think we should do?"

"The same thing you do." I handed her the throwaway cell phone Amy had given me when I was kidnapped.

She made the call. " Hello, is this the FBI? I saw that Mafia boss from New Jersey, Dominic De Marco.

He is not dead. I had a conversation with him. He is staying at 2020 Sunshine Way in St. Petersburg, Florida. His sister, Louise, who is supposed to be dead, is with him. She goes by the name of Denise Madison. Dominic is only here long enough to get new credentials. It doesn't give you much time."

We locked arms and headed back to the motel. On the way, I smashed the phone with a rock. We put parts of it in several different trash receptacles along the way.

THE END

About the Author

Susan Keene was born in California and raised in Illinois. She spent twenty years in the medical profession and loves to weave her experiences into the books she writes.

Besides helping to create a workshop for beginning writers, she is an officer in Sleuth's Ink Mystery Writers and a member of Ozarks Romance Authors.

She loves speaking to children and young adults about writing as a career. This year she will join the Annual Children's Literary Festival of the Ozarks, held at Missouri State University, as a speaker and mentor.

Keene lives on a farm in the beautiful Ozarks, where she and her family raise cattle, sheep, apples, and pears. Her current work, *Who's Roxie Watkins?* is the second book in her Kate Nash mystery series.